A Hearse of Another Color

KENDELL FOSTER CROSSEN
Writing as
M.E. CHABER

I0663017

STEEGER BOOKS / **2020**

PUBLISHED BY STEEGER BOOKS
Visit steegerbooks.com for more books like this.

PUBLISHING HISTORY

Hardcover
New York: Holt, Rinehart & Co., July 1958.
Toronto: Clarke, Irwin & Co., July 1958.
London: T.V. Boardman (American Bloodhound Mystery #253), March 1959. Dust jacket by Denis McLoughlin.

Paperback
New York: Pocket Books #1259, September 1959. Cover by James Meese.
London: Corgi Books #972, 1961. Cover by James. E. McConnell.
New York: Paperback Library (63-486), A Milo March Mystery, #15, December 1970. Cover by Robert McGinnis.

Magazine
Serialized as "A Hearse of Another Colour" in *Suspense* (UK: Fleetwood Publications), May 1960 (vol. 3, no. 5) and June 1960 (vol. 3, no. 6). Illustrated by W. Langhammer.

ISBN: 978-1-61827-516-5

Milo March is a hard-drinking, womanizing, wisecracking, James-Bondian character. He always comes out on top through a combination of personality, bluff, bravado, luck, skill, experience, and intellect. He is a shrewd judge of human character, a crack shot, and a deeper character than I have found in most of the other spy/thriller novels I've read. But, above all, he is a con-man—and a very good one. It is Milo March himself who makes the series worth reading.

—Don Miller, *The Mystery Nook* fanzine 12

Steeger Books is proud to reissue twenty-three vintage novels and stories by M.E. Chaber, whose Milo March Mysteries deliver mile-a-minute action and breezily readable entertainment for thriller buffs.

Milo is an Insurance Investigator who takes on the tough cases. Organized crime, grand theft, arson, suspicious disappearances, murders, and millions and millions of dollars—whatever it is, Milo is just the man for the job. Or even the only man for it.

During World War II, Milo was assigned to the OSS and later the CIA. Now in the Army Reserves, with the rank of Major, he is recalled for special jobs behind the Iron Curtain. As an agent, he chops necks, trusses men like chickens to steal their uniforms, shoots point blank at secret police—yet shows compassion to an agent from the other side.

Whatever Milo does, he knows how to do it right. When the work is completed, he returns to his favorite things: women, booze, and good food, more or less in that order....

THE MILO MARCH MYSTERIES

For Lisa

"Come, beloved, let me lift you to the heavens
That you may read what's written on yonder star."

CONTENTS

ONE

It was one of those days when nothing happened. I'd been having too many of them recently. I sat around the office all day and the phone rang only once. Then it was the phone company wanting to know when I was going to pay my bill. I told them I'd take it up with my board of directors and hung up.

Sometimes that's the way it is in my business. The name is March. Milo March. I'm an insurance investigator. With my own office—March's Insurance Service Corporation—on Madison Avenue, that little section of New York famous for strong martinis and neat women. I'm for hire. Any insurance company that wants to pay the freight of a hundred dollars a day and expenses has me for the asking. I go out and solve their little problems and usually save them a bundle of loot. And you, too, for the premiums you pay on your insurance depend partly on how much is stolen from the insurance companies.

But don't make a big thing out of it and confuse me with those private eyes that wander around on your television screen. I wear a trench coat when it's raining. I carry a gun when somebody is trying to shoot me. I chase women sometimes, but only when they get that chase-me look in their eyes.

Finally it was late enough in the day so that I knew there wouldn't be any business calls. All the vice-presidents would be in the nearest pub. I locked the office and went down to the Blue Mill on Commerce Street in the Village. I had a couple of dry martinis and a steak. After coffee I went home to my apartment on Perry Street with the idea of curling up with a good book.

I had a glass of Canadian Club in my left hand and was just opening the book with my right hand when there was a knock on my door. I put the book down, took a quick drink from the glass so it wouldn't get lonesome while I was gone, and went to the door. I opened it, ready to say that I didn't want to buy whatever was being sold, but I never got beyond opening my mouth. It stayed that way.

She was tall, maybe five seven. Short blond hair that curled around her head like golden feathers. Blue eyes that looked like the Pacific on a spring day. And a figure that would have made Jayne Mansfield look like an underfed waif.

"Please," she said. "May I come in for a minute?" What could I say? I held the door open and she slipped past me, her perfume reaching out to tug at my senses. I closed the door and turned to face her.

"I'm sorry," she said, "but some man has been following me and I didn't know what to do, so I knocked on the first door I came to."

"He followed you into the building?" I asked.

She nodded. "I came in to see a friend on the floor below and the man followed. My friend wasn't home and I was afraid to go back down, so I came on up here. I hope you don't mind."

"Perish the thought," I said fervently. I was about to ask who her friend was but then realized I didn't know any of my neighbors, so it didn't make any difference.

"Personally I'm in favor of having open house. At least now. I was just having a small drink of Canadian Club. Will you join me?"

She hesitated only a minute. "I would love it," she said. "With only a little water, please."

I fixed her a drink and brought it to her. Then I picked up my own. "Here's to the happy accident that brought you knocking at my door," I said.

She smiled at me over the rim of her glass.

"As long as I'm providing the sanctuary, perhaps we ought to introduce ourselves. I'm Milo March."

"My name is Lisette. Lisette Smith."

"A fine old name," I said gravely, but I knew she was lying about the Smith part. Maybe she had a good reason. She didn't know anything about me except that I'd been willing to hide her in my apartment, which probably put me in a class with damn near the entire male population.

"It's very kind of you to let me come in here."

"Kind?" I said. "It's just that I have good eyesight."

There was a knock on the door.

"Maybe that's the man," she said.

I looked at her and realized there was real fear in her eyes. "You go into the bedroom," I told her, "so he won't see you when I open the door, and I'll take care of him."

She took her drink and walked into the bedroom. I watched her. She was just as pretty going as she was coming. There was another knock on the door. I went over and opened it.

He was a heavyset man wearing a wrinkled blue suit and a battered hat. He stood as if his feet were tired, and the expression on his face said that he didn't give a damn who knew it.

"You seen anything of a tall, blond girl?" he asked.

"Practically all of her," I said. "Let me see, it was over in Jersey City at the burlesque house and her name was—"

"Funny guy," he grunted. "Did a tall, blond girl come into your apartment within the last few minutes?"

"Do I look like the kind of guy who would answer the door if one had?" I said.

"I'll take a look," he said.

"Not tonight, buster. I don't like strange men wandering through my apartment. Besides, you're not my type. Go take a brisk stroll for yourself before you get hurt and I have to call the cops to sweep you up."

"Just whisper," he said. He reached in his pocket and pulled out a badge. "You want to make a Supreme Court case out of it, I'll take you in, too."

Well, that did make it look a little different. And maybe that was the explanation of why the girl lied. I wouldn't help her by fighting the police force. I stepped away from the door and he walked in. He stood there, sniffing the air.

"Where is she?" he asked.

"I don't know what you're talking about," I said. I wasn't going to obstruct justice, but I wasn't going to help him either.

"There's perfume in this room," he said.

"I always dab a little behind my ears when somebody knocks. One never knows who's going to be there."

"Wise guys," he said. "I get a bellyful of them."

"Is that what makes it stick out that way?" I asked.

He just grunted and walked into the kitchen, snapping on the light. He looked around, even opening the closet. Then he walked out and headed for the bedroom. I followed him. He snapped on the light in bedroom and I wondered why he didn't say anything. I reached the doorway and found out. She wasn't in sight. There were two closets in the bedroom. He looked in both of them, pushing my suits to one side. No girl. I'd already discovered the reason why. The bedroom window was open. There was a fire escape outside. He discovered it about the same time. He went over and looked out.

"You always leave this window open like this?" he asked, turning back to me.

"I like a lot of fresh air," I said.

"Sure," he grunted. "What did you say your name was?"

"Milo March."

"Yeah? Well, keep your nose clean, March, or I may see you downtown yet." He went out of the apartment fast and hurried down the stairs.

I went over and closed the door. Then I went back into the bedroom. I went over and looked out the window, looking up as well as down. There wasn't a thing to see, but I thought maybe she was hiding somewhere. I whistled softly, but it didn't bring any response.

Finally I closed the window. I looked around the bedroom. There was no sign of the glass of whiskey. I guessed she'd taken it with her—the frugal type.

I went into the other room and finished my own drink. I

tried to read the book again, but I kept thinking about the blonde. And not just because she'd taken one of my best glasses.

TWO

When I awakened the next morning there was nothing but the missing glass to prove that she had ever be there. That and the memory of how she looked. I was still curious, and I decided I'd see what I could find out. I made myself some breakfast and went up to the office. Then I called a friend of mine on the police force.

"Do me a favor," I said. "You know where I live on Perry Street. Last night there was a cop after a tall, blond girl in that neighborhood. He was even in my building. I'd like to know what it was all about."

"What's the cop's name and what precinct was he from?"

"He didn't say and I never got around to asking him."

"Milo, you're slipping," he said. "Well, I'll see what I can do. Where are you?"

"The office."

"I'll call you back," he said and hung up.

I sat around and fiddled with the morning mail—all of it bills. I opened the desk drawer, told myself firmly that it was too early for a drink, and closed it again. Finally, forty-five minutes later, the phone rang. I scooped it up.

"Yeah?" I said.

"Milo," my friend said, "I'm afraid you've been taken in by a tin badge."

"What do you mean?" I asked.

"There wasn't any kind of rumble on Perry Street last night. I checked with the local precinct, the Detective Bureau, Narcotics, Homicide, and even the Special Service Squad. No detective was around there last night—at least officially. And nobody was looking for a tall, blond girl unless it was his own."

I cursed with feeling.

"You're getting old, son," he said. "Letting the light from a tin badge blind you. That's not like the Milo I knew. Well, I'll see you around, kid." He hung up.

I put the receiver back on the hook and cursed some more. He was right. It wasn't like me. I knew what had done it. The guy had looked so much like a tired cop that I hadn't even looked closely at the badge. But that was no excuse. I wondered if the girl got away all right, then decided there was no way for me to find out.

The phone rang. I picked it up and said hello.

"Milo, boy, how are you?" a voice asked. "This is Martin Raymond."

It was a welcome voice because it probably meant a job. He was the vice-president of Intercontinental Insurance, a company that hired me pretty often.

"I'm fine," I said. "And how are all your little premiums?"

"Got some spare time, Milo?"

"Well," I said, "I was supposed to go up with the next satellite, but I suppose I can put that off. They're getting to be like streetcars."

He laughed just to show he appreciated me. "Can you run over here?"

"If it's all right for me to walk, I'll be there in ten minutes."

"See you, boy," he said and hung up.

I called my phone answering service and told them to take over. Then I went out and walked up Madison Avenue until I came to the Intercontinental building. Upstairs in the fancy reception room there was a redheaded receptionist with a personality like the Monroe Doctrine—Marilyn, that is. When you stood over her desk it was like looking down the Grand Canyon, only more fun. I stalled as long as I could and then told her who I wanted to see. She consulted with the telephone.

"You may go right in, Mr. March," she said with a smile.

"Thanks, honey," I said. "And whatever you do, don't let them turn you into a secretary or typist."

"Why?" she wanted to know.

"It gives me confidence in the stability of Intercontinental to see you out here," I said gravely. "Besides, I shudder to think what might happen if you leaned over an electric typewriter."

"Oh, you," she said, but I noticed that she unconsciously took a deep breath and held it. I admired the results for a minute, then went on back to Raymond's office. His secretary waved me on in.

"Glad you could make it," he said as I came in.

"Wasn't sure I could," I said. "I lost the gunbearers back by the redhead, but I pushed on through."

He laughed, but his mind wasn't on it. "Think you can take on a small job for us, Milo?"

"How small? If it's one of those ten-minute jobs, the price goes up."

"Shouldn't take you more than three or four days to clear this one up," he said.

"Guess I can," I said. Even three or four hundred dollars would be better than what I was jingling in my pocket at the moment. "Where is it?" I asked. The last two jobs I'd done for them had taken me out of the country.*

"New Orleans."

"A nice place," I said, thinking what I could do with an expense account there. "What's the case?"

"It's a bit screwy," he grunted. "But despite the unusual circumstances surrounding the beginning, we thought it sounded all right. Three men, all of whom carried regular policies with us, went to New Orleans to hunt for ancient pirate treasure. A silly thing for grown men to do, but it was their business."

"Jean Laffite?"** I asked.

"Something like that. They claimed to have a map and all sorts of guides as to how to find the treasure."

"Don't tell me," I said, "that Intercontinental is now insuring treasure hunts."

"Of course not," he snapped. "The men wanted life insurance policies, each one payable to the survivor or survivors of their expedition, each policy to be in force only until they returned. We issued the policies. They were all three responsible businessmen and there seemed to be very little risk in it."

---

* See *A Lonely Walk* (Italy) and *The Gallows Garden* (the Caribbean Islands) by M.E. Chaber.
** Jean Laffite was a famous American pirate, active in and around New Orleans in the 19th century. Legend had it that he had buried stolen treasures such as gold coins in various places along the Texas and Louisiana coast. Many have searched, but I cannot find a verified claim to have found any, even to this day.

"Let me guess," I said. "Cynical old man that I am. One of the three buccaneers is dead and the other two want to collect. Only you think they may have bumped him off and the treasure they were really hunting is the one in your bank account."

"It's worse than that," he said gloomily. "Two of them have vanished and the third man claims they are dead."

"How much?"

"Each policy was for fifty thousand."

"A hundred grand. A tidy little sum."

"A hundred and fifty thousand altogether," he said. "Each man carried another twenty-five thousand of regular insurance."

"Better tell me more."

"The three men," he said, "were John Bryant, Peter Lane, and Herman Mack. Bryant and Mack are the two presumably dead. The story as we get it from the New Orleans police is that the three of them went to an island where their map indicated there was treasure. Lane, the survivor, claims that he was separated from the other two. It was night. Then Lane heard a scream and went searching for them, but never found them. He claims that he thinks they were caught in quicksand."

"The bodies?" I asked.

"Not found yet," he said. "It leaves us with four choices. The men met death accidentally, as Lane claims. Somebody unknown killed them and disposed of the bodies. Lane killed the two men and disposed of the bodies, either to collect the insurance or get possession of the treasure they found and collect the insurance. Or the three men entered into a conspiracy in which the two would disappear and the third would collect for the three of them. We want to know which of the four possibilities is correct."

"New Orleans cops?" I asked.

"They haven't turned up anything. They haven't arrested Lane, but they have requested that he not leave the city, which indicates they are not yet satisfied with his story."

"He made a claim yet?"

"Not a formal claim, but he did notify us that he thought they were dead. We presume that this is preliminary to making a claim."

I nodded. "All the men have families?"

"Yes. Wives and children."

"That makes it sound less like a conspiracy," I said. "What about their financial pictures?"

"Good, according to our preliminary investigations. All three men were in the twenty to twenty-five thousand dollar bracket."

"The vice-president league," I said.

"Well ..." he said uncomfortably. "Bryant was in market research, Mack was in publicity, and I seem to recall that Lane is an account executive in advertising."

"Wouldn't you know it?" I said. "Characters like that and they have to go out looking for pirate treasure. If they wanted adventure, why the hell didn't they just take mistresses and let it go at that? Although I suppose you wouldn't insure them in that case."

"Moral turpitude," he murmured.

"Turpitude is something used to thin paint on Madison Avenue," I said. "You give me a pain—and don't make me say where. Moral turpitude! There isn't one of you characters who could pass your own moral turpitude test."

"You're being a little extreme," he said.

"Am I?" I asked. "What about that blond secretary you were keeping in an apartment last year?"

"Well, that … ," he began stiffly. Then suddenly he relaxed and grinned at me. "She was pretty nice, wasn't she?"

"Yummy," I agreed. "I'm glad that you can be human. And that takes care of moral turpitude—I hope."

"I wonder what became of her," he said dreamily.

"Down, boy," I told him. "Not on company time. Let's get back to the case. Why are you in such a sweat if they haven't found the bodies?"

"Naturally," he said, "we will not pay until they are found. But we'd like to get a jump on the case while it's still warm. It's better than trying to pick it up a year from now—or seven years."

"It's your money and I like it. When do you want me to start?"

"At once."

"The usual hundred a day and expenses?" I asked.

He nodded. "But try to go easy on the expenses, Milo. The board wasn't too happy the last time."

I told him what the board could do, collectively and singly. "They were happy enough about the money I saved them, so tell them not to begrudge a hard-working man one or two martinis on the house. You got anything else for me?"

"That's about it," he said. "You can look at the policy reports, of course, but I've given you everything in them." He looked at the memo pad on his desk. "A Lieutenant Stern of the New Orleans Police has been in charge of the case there. You'll find Peter Lane staying at the Royal House. You want to see the reports?"

"I'll take your word for it," I said. "But there is one more thing I want."

"I know," he said wearily. "How much?"

"Five hundred is a nice round number to start with," I told him. "You know I always return anything left over."

"Yeah, but there's never anything left over."

"Can I help it if you only assign me to expensive cases?"

"You ought to try another case," he said. "Like Imperial instead of Canadian Club."

I stared at him round-eyed. "Oh, you made a funny. Or did you hear it someplace last night?"

He just grinned and buzzed for his secretary. He sent her for the money. While we waited for her to return, I had to sit and listen to his latest triumphs in the Fairfield County set. But finally the girl came back with five crisp bills, each one bearing the beautiful number 100 on it. I tucked them lovingly into my pocket, assured Raymond that he'd hear from me and left.

I went back to my office, checked in with the answering service, and had a drink from the bottle in the desk drawer just by way of celebrating. Then I checked up on getting to New Orleans. I found I could catch a late-night plane that would get me there in time for breakfast. I made a reservation. I also called and made a reservation at the Royal House. Then I phoned Raymond and told him when I was going and where I'd be staying.

After that there wasn't much to do. I let the answering service know that I'd be away for a few days. I went over and picked up my flight ticket. Then I took a cab down to my apartment in the Village. I packed my suitcase and after that the rest of the day was mine. I went out and invested part of those big bills in very dry martinis. After the second one, it seemed like the best investment I'd ever made.

After spending the afternoon in such boyish pleasures, I had dinner, a few more drinks, and went home to pick up my suitcase. I took a cab to the airport and checked in at the counter. As soon as the gate was open, I was through and was the first one to board the big plane. I found my seat and relaxed, closing my eyes.

I didn't open them until after I felt the plane take to the air. Even then it was something else that made me sit up. I couldn't figure out what it was at first. I looked around. The plane was about half filled with passengers. I looked above the door in front and the *No Smoking* sign was off. I lit a cigarette. It was then that I noticed there was a blond girl sitting in front of me. Then I knew what it was that had made me open my eyes. It was her perfume. There was something familiar about it.

Just to make sure, I got up and went to the men's room in the front of the plane. On the way back I got a good look at her. It was the same blonde. I dropped into the seat beside her.

"Don't let anybody tell you it isn't a small world," I said.

"In fact, it's already so small that if it will only stop spinning, I may get off."

She looked at me. There was recognition in her eyes all right, but there was something else, too—maybe fear.

"I'm not following you," I said, "if that's what you're about to start thinking. Not that I would mind following you, but I wouldn't have known where to start."

"Hello," she said. "It's Mr. March, isn't it?"

"I prefer Milo," I said.

"You must have thought me awfully rude," she said. "I'm afraid I didn't get a chance to thank you for last night."

"For which part? I'm sorry, honey, I thought the guy was the real goods. It was only this morning I discovered he was a phony cop. I gave myself twenty lashes on the bare back for being a jerk. I gather you got away all right."

She smiled. "Yes, I'm afraid that I was rather frightened. I went out the window as soon as you went to the door. As soon as I reached the corner I found a cab."

"I hope your drink was properly mixed," I said politely.

"Oh," she said. "I did take your glass with me, didn't I? I finished the drink before I reached the cab, but I'm afraid I left the glass somewhere on the street. I'm so sorry."

"It's all right," I said gallantly. "I don't need glasses. I can see you all right with the naked eye. In fact, if I could see you any better, I don't think I could stand it."

She laughed. It proved she had a kind heart. "You're going to New Orleans?" she asked.

"Yes"

"Vacation?"

"On business," I said, "but I expect to have some pleasure, too."

"What business are you in?" she asked. She didn't really care, but she was going to make conversation because of the night before.

"Insurance," I said. "I'm what you might call an adjuster. Somebody gets knocked off and I go around and make sure that the beneficiary didn't do the knocking, and then the company pays off."

"Oh," she said, looking at me, "that sounds terribly exciting. You're going to New Orleans on a case?"

"Yeah," I said. I wasn't going to make any secret about my business in New Orleans, but that didn't mean I was going into all the details. "What about you? Vacation?"

"No, I live in New Orleans. I've been visiting in New York."

"You live there?" I said. "Maybe that's great—that is, if you'll show me around the town."

She hesitated, but not long. "I guess I do owe you something for last night," she said. "I'll make a bargain with you … Milo. I'll show you New Orleans and you'll tell me about your exciting work."

"It's more exciting when I'm not working," I said, "but it's a bargain. We start with dinner tomorrow night?"

"All right."

I flagged a passing hostess and ordered two drinks. I lit a couple of cigarettes for us and leaned back. Maybe New Orleans was going to be even better than I had anticipated.

"I—I have a confession to make," the blonde said after our drinks had been served.

"Uh-huh," I said. "You're name isn't Smith."

She looked startled. "How did you know?"

"It's true there are a lot of Smiths in the country," I said, "but you'd be surprised how many people one runs into who aren't named Smith. Besides, you hesitated last night before you got it out."

She laughed nervously. "It was silly of me, I know. But I had just picked your apartment at random and I didn't know you, and I guess I was frightened. If you knew, why didn't you say something?"

"I thought you'd tell me when you were ready," I said.

"It's Dufresne," she said. "The Lisette part was real."

"Pretty," I said. "Creole?"

"Yes," she said proudly. "You know what it means?"

"Sure," I said. "Even Yankees sometimes know something. It means you're descended from the early French settlers of New Orleans. It also means that like every Creole you are— how did they say it?—*sortie de la cuisse de Jupiter.* A piece from the thigh of Jupiter."

"You are surprising," she said. "Where did you learn that?"

"I don't remember," I said. "Probably in a bar somewhere. It's surprising the education that can be picked up in a bar."

We talked for a couple more hours and then both of us took a nap.

It was daylight when the plane circled over New Orleans getting ready to land. I leaned over and looked out the window as it banked. The Mississippi River looked like a giant sluggish serpent, the city of New Orleans caught in one of its coils. Which in a way, I thought, was true since so much of the city is below the river level and subject to the whims of the river.

As the big plane floated closer to the airport, in the distance I could begin to make out some of the old buildings that gave New Orleans its charm, many of them almost side by side with shining new office buildings. It was years since I'd been there, but it seemed almost like coming back to an old friend.

When we landed, there was someone there to meet Lisette. She gave me her address and I promised to call for her that evening. Then I took a cab to the hotel. It turned out to have been a good choice. It was just luxurious enough to make me feel that I was spending Intercontinental's money wisely. When I got to my room I called room service and told them to send up a pot of coffee, a bottle of Canadian Club, and a bucket of ice. It was still too early to start working. I'd have some coffee, a couple of drinks, and maybe grab a couple more hours of sleep.

The boy delivered the coffee and the whiskey and departed a dollar happier. I got partly undressed, and poured a cup of coffee for my left hand and a Canadian Club on the rocks for my right hand. Then I made myself comfortable. There's nothing in the world quite like New Orleans coffee; It almost stands up by itself, which is just the way I like it.

The phone rang. Thinking it was the desk wanting to be sure that I was happy, I picked up the receiver and said, "Yeah?"

"Mr. March?" a man's voice asked.

"Yeah," I said. I didn't like it. This didn't sound like the desk and I didn't think that anybody knew I was in New Orleans.

"This is Lieutenant Stern of the New Orleans Police," the voice said. That made it a little better, but not enough. "Sorry to bother you, but I thought you would be checked in by now. Are you planning on dropping in to see me this morning?"

"I was, but not quite this early in the morning. Do all the New Orleans cops go to work so early?"

He laughed. "I'm on the early shift this week. I have some work to do this morning, so why don't you come down to see me in about two hours? I should be free by then. And that will give you the chance to have some coffee and relax."

"I was just about to do that," I told him. "Glad you called. I'll drop down in a couple of hours."

"Fine."

"Just one thing more, Lieutenant ..."

"Yes?"

"How did you know I was coming and that I would be at this hotel?"

"Your office sent me a wire," he said. "Why?"

"Nothing," I said. "I guess I'm just careful. I like to know why people know where I am. Okay. I'll see you later."

"Good," he said and hung up. I went back to work on the coffee.

It was about ten minutes later and I was switching from coffee to Canadian Club when there was a knock on the door. I put down my glass and went to the door. I swung it open, expecting to see a bellboy.

He was something different. He was a small, trim little

man, his suit neat and expensive. His hair was dark, as was his face, and his full lips were spread in a smile that wasn't a smile. But it was his eyes that were the giveaway. They held nothing but sight. They stared at me as if I were a piece of furniture and he were the upholsterer who had come to give an estimate. He was something international; you could find one like him anywhere in the world where there was a quick buck to be made if you didn't care how you made it. I didn't even have to look to see the slight bulge under his left arm. It was just as much standard equipment as his hair.

"You Milo March?" he asked flatly. Without waiting for an answer, he pushed into the room. It wasn't obvious and I didn't have to move but it was still a push.

"I'm Milo March," I said. "Why don't you come in?"

"Funny," he said. He closed the door. His gaze went over the room like a germicide looking for a germ. It swung back to me with a clear and unpleasant implication. "Very funny. You got any other funny lines?"

"I forgot to bring my writers with me," I said. "I didn't know you were auditioning. But you've left something out."

"What?"

"You," I said. "Don't tell me you're the latest version of the Welcome Wagon. What happened to all the nice old ladies? But if you are, just give me my free package of Wheaties and beat it. I'm sure you have a busy schedule."

"Funny," he said again.

"You're repeating yourself," I told him. "Okay. Let's stop the ad-libs. You got a name or do you just go by a number?"

"Don't get too funny," he said.

"Why should I?" I asked wearily. "Haven't you heard? Comedians are out this season. Westerns are the big thing. While we're waiting for the trend to change, you might tell me your name. I don't like to talk to people I don't know."

"Eddie Capo," he said.

"A pretty name," I admitted, "if you like the type. I don't think I do. You got business here, or did you just drop in to welcome me because the Chamber of Commerce is busy?"

"Yeah, I got business here," he said tonelessly, "but you ain't. I dropped in to tell you to take the next plane back to New York."

THREE

The fast money boys are always the same, in New York, Rome, or New Orleans. They walk in and give their orders and that's supposed to be it. I've run into a lot of them and I know how they tick. But I hadn't expected to run into any of them on this job. It was a simple insurance case—only now maybe it wasn't so simple. I looked at Eddie Capo with interest.

"Who do you work for, Eddie?" I asked.

"Who said I worked for anybody?" he countered.

"Okay, we'll try it a different way. Why should I take the next plane back to New York?"

"You're a nice guy," he said, only his heart wasn't in it. "The climate up there is better for you. I just got a feeling that New Orleans ain't a very healthy place for you."

"You were just walking by the hotel and you got the feeling that there was a nice guy who had just checked into the hotel and maybe he had an allergy to New Orleans, and you considered it your Christian duty to stop in and warn him. Is that how it goes?"

"Yeah."

"And did your feelings also tell you that the nice guy's name was Milo March?"

"Maybe they did."

"It's mighty neighborly of you, neighbor," I said. "I get

feelings like that, too. In fact, you might say that I'm the seventh son of a seventh son and can read the future. And I have a feeling that this room is going to be unhealthy for you in about two minutes. You might even break out in all kinds of lumps."

He stared at me without expression.

"I hope," I said, "that I'm not losing anything in translation, but that means get out. Now."

"I could take you," he said. Something like excitement was stirring in his black eyes.

"Maybe," I said. "Then again, maybe you couldn't. But I'll also bet you don't have any orders about trying, and a well-trained rat doesn't squeak unless he's been told to."

The expression in his eyes got a little stronger, but he didn't make a move and I knew I was right.

"Outside, buster," I told him. "And tell your boss, whoever he is, not to send a boy to do a man's work. I don't like to be pushed. When it happens, I usually push back."

He walked to the door and opened it. He looked back at me and the eagerness was still there even though he was holding it back. "I got a feeling," he said, "that I'll be seeing you again, so you'd better keep your nose clean."

"Send me a box of Kleenex," I said. "Monogrammed. Now—out. Close the door gently. I have delicate ears."

He said a short, hard word under his breath and closed the door. I went back to my drink. I wondered where Eddie Capo fit into the picture and had Martin Raymond sent him a telegram, too. Or maybe there was a leak in Lieutenant Stern's nice little police department. But there wasn't much I could do about it at the moment, so I finished my drink and went to sleep for an hour.

I got up and took a fast shower. Then I went downstairs and had another cup of coffee. After that I grabbed a cab and told the driver to take me to police headquarters.

Lieutenant Stern turned out to be about fifty, a big, smooth-faced man who looked like a dozen other cops I knew. I've often wondered whether it's that certain types of men are attracted to the force and do well on it, or whether the job shapes the men after they've been there a number of years.

"Glad to see you, March," he said, shaking my hand. There was just a hint of Southern accent. "As I told your office when this happened a couple of weeks ago, I'll be glad to give you all the cooperation I can."

"Fine," I said. I lit a cigarette and stared at him over the tip of it. "How many guys you got in here who are also on the payroll of somebody who's on the wrong side of the fence?"

He didn't get it at first. When he did, the color slid up over his face like someone pulling a red window shade the wrong way. He gripped his desk and for a minute I wasn't sure but what he was going to come right over the top of it.

"What the hell do you mean?" he asked.

"You know a little hood named Eddie Capo?" I asked.

"I know him."

"Well, about two minutes after you called this morning, Eddie Capo visited me to say that New Orleans wasn't healthy for me. Now, so far as I know, Martin Raymond notified you that I would be at that hotel, but nobody else knew it."

He sat back in his chair and the color left his face but the grimness didn't. "There are no crooked cops on my squad," he said.

"Okay," I said. I grinned at him. "I'm sorry, Lieutenant, to be so rough on you right away. But I wanted to be sure that you yourself weren't the leak and that's why I threw it at you. Now I know you aren't. But don't be too sure there isn't a leak somewhere around here. It's happened a lot of places, and Eddie Capo didn't look like the sort of citizen Martin Raymond would notify."

"Damn you, March," he said. "You almost got slugged."

"I know," I said. "Sometimes that's the only way you can tell an honest cop from a crooked one without spending too much time on it. You're liable to get slugged either way, but it's the way the slugging is done that tips it. And I told you I'm sorry."

"Okay," he said gruffly. "I'd be willing to swear by every man in here, but I'll check them all through anyway. And if that's the way you work, I guess you'll get along all right. What else did Eddie Capo have to say?"

"That was about it. He thought I ought to leave town, and I couldn't see it that way. An honest difference of opinion. I noticed he was carrying some artillery."

"He has a permit," the Lieutenant said curtly. "So Eddie just walked away quietly when you told him to?"

"Yeah. But to be honest, I don't think it was all because of me. I think he had orders not to push it too far. Yet."

"How about you?" Stern asked. "You carrying a gun, too?"

I shook my head. "But if things get too rough, I may be around asking for a permit."

"Why should they get too rough on you?"

"I don't intend to just sit around and watch you sweat," I said. "I won't step on any toes unless I have to, and if I turn up anything, your department can have all the credit. But I'm going to work."

"Damnit, the whole thing is getting full of amateurs," he said. "Sorry, I didn't really mean that to apply to you. I'm sure that you're a professional in your field."

"It's okay, Lieutenant. I told you I'm not interested in credit. I get paid in cash. Now, where does Eddie Capo fit into this?"

"Damned if I know," he admitted. "I haven't been working on any angle that would have Eddie in it. That opens up other possibilities."

"Such as?"

"I'm not sure. Yeah, I know what Eddie is. It's written all over him. And he's done time up North; I checked on that. But he's never been gotten for anything down here. Oh, he's been pulled in. I've questioned him a couple of times myself. But nothing's been pinned on him."

"Who's he work for?"

"I don't know. He stays pretty much alone. I know as well as you do that he has to work for somebody. He's not smart enough to be on his own. But I don't know of any tie-ups."

"What's he suspected of?"

"Almost everything in the book. Even the Federals have been after him a couple of times on suspicion of bringing narcotics into the country, or having them brought in. But they couldn't pin anything on him, so maybe he's in something else."

"What do you think?"

He shrugged. "The Feds say there's a lot of narcotics coming in through New Orleans."

"Is there?"

"How the hell do I know?" he demanded angrily. "I work in Homicide and that's all I know. ... But they're probably right."

"Do I get a permit if I need it?"

"I guess it could be done," he said.

"Okay," I said. "Let's get back to our case and find out about Eddie when the time comes. What's the story on the two guys who vanished into the wild blue yonder?"

He swore again. "I don't know why all the damn fools in the world have to come down here to hunt pirate treasure. I guess you know that's what the three men came here for. They had a map that one of them had dug up somewhere and they hired a guide and a diviner."

"What's a diviner?" I asked.

"He finds the treasure. Some of them use electronic devices now. Others still use a forked stick, various old books, and a variety of fancy spells. They all add up to the same thing."

"What about the two guys they hired?"

"All right, so far as we know," he said. "The guide was Narcisse Coillon. He comes from an old Creole family but didn't get the money. He's been acting as a guide for several years now and we've never had anything against him. His diviner this time was a black boy named Willie Morell. Nothing against him either. He works as a diviner about three or four months a year, then goes off somewhere—probably to blow in his money. He comes back, I guess, when he's broke."

"Okay," I said. "Go ahead."

"Well, the map these three men had showed that the treasure was on Placide Island."

"An island," I interrupted, "and it's still within your jurisdiction?"

"Yeah. I got everything within my jurisdiction. This one is just a small island. Nobody lives on it or could. There's nothing there but swamp, a few grubby trees, and a lot of quicksand."

"Okay."

"They went there two weeks ago at night, the three men, the guide, and the diviner. They went at night because the diviner said that was the best time. Anyway, they landed on the island and started exploring it. According to the story, which the guide and the diviner back up, the method was too slow for two of the men—Bryant and Mack. They wanted to strike out the other way on their own to circle the island and meet Lane, the guide, and the diviner on the other side. Lane claims he tried to stop them, and the guide warned them about quicksand. But they insisted and did take off on their own. It was about a half hour later that Lane heard one of them shout. He stopped looking for treasure and went searching for them. He never found them."

"How did they get to the island?" I asked.

"Hired a boatman. Fellow named West Carroll. Also all right as far as we know. He has a fishing boat and takes out fishing parties and skin-diving parties. Does a lot of skin diving himself. Also takes tourists around when he's free. He stayed on the boat that night. He heard the shout but didn't pay any attention—thought maybe they'd found some treasure."

"Lane says he thinks they got caught in the quicksand and died that way?"

He nodded. "And Coillon, the guide, thinks that's what happened, too."

"What do you think?"

"I don't know," he confessed. "It's possible. There's a lot of quicksand on that island. And you'd go down fast if you got caught in it. We tried probing in most of the places with poles and didn't find anything. But that doesn't mean too much."

"Suppose they're not there?"

"Well," he said, "I did kind of favor this Peter Lane, but I haven't gotten anywhere with him. But I can't figure out why anybody else would want to kill the two men. They didn't know anyone in New Orleans."

"Lane have the chance?"

"Both Coillon and the diviner swear that they were with him all the time. But I figure that doesn't rule him out. It's always possible that he could have bought them, or that he hired someone to get rid of Bryant and Mack."

"Yeah," I said. "How would they get rid of the bodies?"

"Could just sink them in the quicksand."

"There ought to be a law against it," I said dryly. "What about this? Suppose the two men just wanted to vanish and then have their friend Lane claim that something had happened to them. Could they have gotten off the island without anyone knowing it?"

"Not by motorboat," he said. "Carroll would have heard the

motor. But I guess they could have. They could have had a rowboat hidden there or arranged for someone to meet them in a rowboat. It was night and nobody would have seen them. You think that's what happened?"

"No," I admitted, "but it's a possibility. Men will do a lot of things for a hundred thousand dollars. Now another thing. What could be hidden on that island that nobody would want them to find?"

"Pirate treasure, I suppose," he said bitterly. "Every once in a while somebody does find some old Spanish coins around here, and it's enough to give everybody the fever for the next five or ten years."

"Not pirate treasure," I said. "What else?"

"Not a damn thing. You'll realize it when you see the island. You couldn't hide a tin can there and not expect it to be found. Not enough shrubbery on it to hide a bird. Besides, if anyone wanted to keep them off, he would have done something about Lane, the guide, and the diviner."

"Maybe the two men stumbled onto something."

"Nothing to stumble on, except a little swamp grass and a few snakes."

"Okay, then answer me this," I said. "Why are Eddie Capo and whoever he works for so anxious to stop me from trying to find out what happened to the two men?"

"I can give you several answers to that," he said. "Maybe all of them wrong. Eddie Capo might think you're here for another reason—something else he's mixed up in. Did he mention this case?"

"No," I admitted.

"Then, if we want to think that Lane had something done to his two partners, maybe it was arranged through Eddie Capo. Or, taking your guess that maybe they wanted to vanish, it might have been done with Capo's help."

"I suppose so," I said. "I guess Eddie could be bought cheap enough to leave a handsome profit out of a hundred grand. But I don't like it."

"Why?"

"I don't know," I said. "Maybe it's because Eddie looks so much a professional that I think he must be involved in something bigger. Maybe I'm wrong. I have been once or twice in my life."

"I can pull Eddie Capo in and question him," the Lieutenant said, but he didn't sound as if he believed it was going to produce miracles.

"I'd rather you didn't," I said. "Let's give him a little more rope. Maybe he'll hang himself—or me. In the meantime, I'll start nosing around, if you don't mind."

"I don't mind—up to a point," he said. "But don't try to be a cop, too."

"I never do," I said. "I work in my own way, but if somebody has to be arrested, I always yell for the bluecoats. I'm a firm believer in law and order."

He grunted.

"But if things get tough, I'll still want that permit," I said.

"We'll see," he said. "You brought a gun with you?"

"No," I admitted, "but I can always buy one. I thought this was just a simple insurance case with no complications. I didn't know there were going to be any Eddie Capos in it. So

I left the gun home in the dresser drawer."

"You'll let me know what you're doing?" he asked.

"Sure." I grinned at him. "Up to a point. But don't worry. If I dig up anything, you'll get it. And you can have all the credit on anything. Well, I guess that's it for this time."

The door opened and a policeman in his shirt sleeves came into the office. He carried a yellow envelope in his hand. He glanced briefly at me.

"Excuse me, Lieutenant," he said, "but this just came for you and I thought it might be important." He handed the envelope to the Lieutenant and left the office.

Stern tore open the envelope and read the message, his face expressionless. Then he looked at me. "What were you saying?" he asked.

"I was about to say good-bye and thanks," I told him.

"Maybe you'd like to see this," he said. He flipped the yellow message across the desk. It was a telegram. I smoothed it out and read it.

IF MILO MARCH COMES INTO YOUR OFFICE HOLD HIM UNTIL I
GET IN TOUCH WITH YOU STOP THANKS

> JOHN ROCKLAND (LIEUT) BUREAU OF
> SPECIAL SERVICES NEW YORK CITY
> POLICE

FOUR

Now, what the hell did that mean? I wondered. I knew Johnny Rockland very well. He was the cop I'd called the day before to check up on the man who had been following the blonde. What was more important, Johnny knew me. He wasn't the kind of person to pull something like this. Yet there it was. I tossed the telegram back on the desk.

"What is this?" I asked. "A gag?"

"I thought maybe you'd tell me," the Lieutenant said solemnly.

"It has to be," I said. "I know Johnny Rockland very well. I spoke to him on the phone yesterday before I left New York. He's got no reason to do anything like this."

"Hasn't he?"

"No," I said. "Well, it's probably just a joke. I'll be seeing you around, Lieutenant."

"Sure, you will," he said. He must have punched a button on his desk, because the door opened and the same policeman was back.

"Lock him up," the Lieutenant said. "Treat him nicely but be sure the door is still locked."

"Yes, sir," the policeman said.

"Wait a minute," I said. "You can't do this."

"No?" he asked.

"What are you charging me with?" I demanded.

The Lieutenant grinned at me. "You ought to know better than that, March. I can hold you for twenty-four hours on suspicion. If Lieutenant Rockland hasn't gotten in touch by then, I'll charge you with being a material witness."

"Cops," I said bitterly. "If they have a day off, they turn and beat their mothers just to keep in practice."

The cop motioned me through the door and I went. There wasn't much else to do. He took me into the back of the building where there were a number of detention cells. He opened one of them and I walked in. He locked the door.

"Don't go away," he said as he left.

"Cops," I yelled after him. "Bastards, every one of them." But he just kept on going without paying any attention to me.

I looked around; the cell was only about eight feet long and five feet wide, with bars all around. The other cells were empty except for one. That was right next to mine. There was a little unshaven man in it, staring at me with wide eyes.

"What's the matter, Mac?" he asked me.

"Nothing," I snapped. "I just made the mistake of trusting a lousy cop."

He made a clucking noise with his tongue. "They'll do it every time," he said. "You can't trust them, Mac. You go tell one of them something and afore you know it the thing's all over town."

"Yeah," I said. I went over and sat down on the cot.

"What'd they put you in here for, Mac?" the little man asked.

"I told you," I said.

"No," he said. "What did you do to somebody? You know what I mean."

Then I got it. I'd forgotten this was Homicide and that these cells were probably all for people suspected of murder. Not that it made any difference to me.

"What did you do, huh?" he repeated eagerly.

"I killed the King of Poland," I said. I'd been willing to say hello to him, but I didn't want to turn it into a bosom friendship.

"You did?" he said. "I didn't know they had a king. Gee, them Communists got everything, ain't they? You know why they got me in here, Mac?"

"No."

"They say I killed my wife. Ain't so. It's just that she was yelling something fierce and I wanted to sleep. All I did was make her keep quiet. That's all. I tried to tell them."

"Shut up," I said, "or I'll come right through the bars and make you keep quiet the same way you did your wife."

"They wouldn't like it," he said. "They don't like having the cells messed up." But he did go back to his cot and keep quiet.

Not that it did me any good. All the thinking I could do produced nothing but more names for me to call the cops.

I'd been in the cell about an hour when the same cop showed up again. He unlocked the door and motioned me out.

"Has the Lieutenant finally come to his senses and decided to let me go?" I asked.

He shook his head. "Phone call for you. You see, you get all the services of home here." He grinned at me.

I kept all the words under my breath and went with him back down the corridor to the Lieutenant's office. He opened the door and motioned me in. Lieutenant Stern was just getting up from his desk. The phone receiver was lying on the desk, off the hook.

"Phone call for you," he said. He was grinning, too. "I'll wait outside while you take it." He and the other cop went out, closing the door.

I picked up the receiver and said hello.

"Milo, how are you?" the voice asked. "This is Johnny Rockland."

"How the hell do you expect me to be?" I demanded. "What the hell was the idea of sending this cop a telegram telling him to put me in jail?"

"Didn't tell him to put you in jail," Johnny said. He was laughing and I could tell by the sound of it that he wanted to laugh even harder. It didn't help my temper any. "I just asked him to hold you there until I got in touch. I wanted to talk to you and I figured you'd be bound to stop in there and that would be the best way of catching you."

I gave him a short résumé of all the thinking I'd been doing about cops. "And after this," I finished, "say what the hell you want so that an idiot can understand it. If you're going to send messages to cops, you have to use their kind of language."

"Sure, Milo," he said, still laughing. "Anyway, you shouldn't complain too much. You're so lucky that if you fall into the Mississippi while you're down there, you'll probably come up with Queen Isabella's crown jewels around your neck."

"What are you talking about now?" I demanded.

"Remember that guy you checked with me on yesterday? The one who was following the blonde and told you he was a cop?"

"Yeah."

"Think you could describe him?"

"Sure," I said. "He was about five nine or ten, weight probably a hundred and eighty. Dark hair, dark eyes. He wore a crumpled blue suit and a battered brown hat. He walked and stood as though his feet hurt and he had that kind of expression on his face. Just like a cop."

"Yeah. Well, his name is Lew Manton and you must've made him mad the other night."

"Why?"

"One of my boys was going home last night. He has to go along Perry Street. He saw this character entering your building and thought there was something wrong about him. He followed. The guy broke into your apartment and was busy hiding a small package of marijuana cigarettes under the mattress of your bed when he was caught. We figure he was planning to call later to give us an anonymous tip. It might have been a neat enough frame to give you a headache if my boy hadn't been there."

"All right," I said gruffly. "I take back one of the words I said about cops. But not the rest of them."

"We found a phony badge on him when he was searched and a nice little packet of heroin. So we've got him on three counts. This one is a bad boy, Milo. He's got a long record. He's been arrested three times on rape charges and six times on possession of narcotics. He's served three stretches. We've suspected him of being a pusher for some time. But we got him cold on this one and it makes him a fourth offender. I just thought you'd like to know about it."

"Great," I said. "Only the next time you might find a more convenient way of telling me than having me thrown in the cooler."

"Okay, Milo," he said chuckling. "Just wanted you to know we saved you from a bad frame. Sometimes cops are handy to have around."

"Sure, if you don't care who you associate with," I said. "Wait. Don't go away. Since you're spending the taxpayers' money on this call, something good might as well come of it. You know the name Eddie Capo?"

"Yeah, I know the name. Now, there is a tough boy. Haven't heard of him in years, though."

"Well, you're hearing of him now. He's down here. When I got in this morning, he dropped around to tell me that he thought New Orleans might be unhealthy for me."

He whistled. "When does the next plane get into New York? I'll meet you at the airport."

"When did you ever know me to run?" I demanded. "Then you'd better wear your hardware."

"You should have told that to Stern. I'll need a permit down here. What's the picture on Capo?"

"He used to be with Murder, Incorporated. He was one of their triggers. And Dewey's* new broom didn't even touch

---

* Thomas Dewey, as the New York City prosecutor and district attorney, pursued famous members of the assassination-for-hire organization.

him. Oh, he was arrested enough times. I don't have the record here, but I think he was arrested maybe sixteen times on suspicion of murder. He always beat the rap. No witnesses. The one time they thought they had a witness who might nail Capo, the witness took a dive out a hotel window while the cops were guarding him."

"Who does he work for?"

"Well, he always did work for the Syndicate, so it would be a safe guess that he still does."

"But who in the Syndicate?" I asked. "Do me a favor and see if you can find out."

"Okay."

"And don't get me arrested to tell me about it," I said. "I'm at the Royal House. It'll be simpler just to let me know there."

He laughed again. "Okay, Milo. I'll see you. Thank Lieutenant Stern for me."

He hung up before I could comment on that. I put the receiver back on the hook and went and opened the door. Lieutenant Stern was standing just outside. He was still grinning.

"You can have your phone and office back now," I told him.

"Thanks," he said, coming in. "Say, that was funny about misunderstanding that telegram, wasn't it?"

"Very," I said. "I suppose I can go now?"

"Sure. I'm sorry, March, but I guess that kind of makes us even. You gave me a rough time when you first came in."

I started to burn again, but then the humor of the situation finally penetrated. I grinned at him. "Okay, but I want something else thrown in. I want that permit."

"I wasn't that rough on you," he said.

"I won't shoot any cops unless they shoot first," I said, "but Johnny just told me who Capo is. Or was—and I don't suppose he's lost his skill. And I'll look awfully silly if he ever starts shooting at me and all I can do is point my finger and shout 'Bang.' "

"Lieutenant Rockland spoke very highly of you—after he got through laughing," the Lieutenant said, "so I guess maybe it can be done. Come down tomorrow and I'll have it for you. You can pick up a gun near here."

"Good," I said. "I'll see you."

I went out and got a cab and went back to the hotel. It was already lunchtime, so I went into the dining room. I had a couple of quick martinis to soothe my shattered nerves, then had lunch. After lunch, I went out to the house phones and asked the operator to give me Peter Lane's room. She rang, but there was no answer. I went over to the desk.

"Did Mr. Lane say when he'd be back?" I asked the clerk.

"Mr. Lane?" he said. Slowly the vacant look was replaced by one of recognition. "Oh, Mr. Lane. Why, I just saw him go into the bar."

"Thanks," I said. I turned and went into the bar. There were only two people sitting at the bar, one at either end. One of them was a pretty redheaded girl. I took a good look before I decided she wasn't Lane. Then, reluctantly, I turned my gaze to the man. I think I might have recognized him even if the bar had been crowded. He had that Madison Avenue look about him, and it was only partly the Brooks Brothers suit and the Princeton haircut. He also had an Ivy League type face.

Nobody would suspect him of belonging to a minority group. At the moment he was toying with his drink and glancing occasionally at the redhead. He was probably figuring out a new move in checkers—how to jump fifteen bar stools at once.

I went over and sat next to him, on the side toward the redhead. He took a quick glance at me and then forgot about me; he didn't recognize a fellow club member.

"Canadian Club with a little water," I told the bartender. "Only don't drown it."

I waited until the bartender had served me and moved away.

I took a drink; then, without looking around, I said, "You're Peter Lane?"

I could feel him start next to me and I knew he was looking at me.

"Yes," he said finally. "Do I know you?"

"No, but you're going to," I said. "I'm Milo March. I'm down here at the request of Intercontinental Insurance."

"Oh," he said. There was a lot of mixed feeling in that one little word.

"I want to talk to you," I said, looking at him.

"Now?"

"Yes."

He took another glance at the redhead and decided that he'd have to pass it up for the time being. "All right," he said reluctantly. "But I don't understand it. No claims have been put in."

"They will be," I said. "By you as well as others. We like to know what it's all about when it happens."

"The police are quite competent to handle the case," he said. He was just being sullen because he was getting cheated out of a chance to make a pass at the redhead.

"Sure," I said. "Competent, but not as interested as we are. By several thousand dollars."

"I didn't have anything to do with what happened to John and Herman," he said. "My God, they were my friends. We went to school together."

"And one doesn't kill somebody who wears the old school tie, does one?" I said. "You're jumping way ahead, Lane. I didn't say that you had anything to do with it."

"Well, I'm getting a little tired of people thinking I did. The stupid cops seem to think so or they'd let me leave here."

"First they're competent, now they're stupid," I said. "You ought to make up your mind. That shuttle bit will never land the client. You run that up the flagpole and nobody will salute it."

He looked at me and suddenly grinned. "Sorry," he said. "I guess it's got me a bit jumpy. John and Herman were my friends and I feel pretty damn bad about it. What did you say your name was?"

"March. Milo March. And all I want is some information from you."

"Okay," he said. He ran his hand over his short hair. "I'll do my best to help you, of course."

"Good," I said. "For a starter, would you mind telling me just what this pirate treasure bit was?"

"I guess in a way I started it," he said, "although it was

Herman—Mack, that is—who finally pushed all of us to go. My wife likes antiques, so for her last birthday I picked up an old chest in an antique shop. When we opened it, we found this map inside. We figured out that it was a map to pirate treasure down here, but we didn't take it seriously. I first showed it to the boys as a gag and said we ought to go treasure hunting. We used to kid about it every time we had lunch together, which was once or twice a week."

"Until finally it wasn't so much of a joke," I suggested.

"Yes, I guess that's it. But even when we came down, I don't think we really believed we'd find any treasure. Oh, maybe each of us sort of hoped we would—people have found old treasure around here—but we didn't believe it."

"Then why did you come?"

"We talked about it first as a gag, then we started thinking it would make an interesting vacation for the three of us. Give us a lot to talk about when we got back. But it was Herman who finally started pushing it. He was in public relations, you know."

I nodded and signaled to the bartender to give us fresh drinks.

"Herman began to get the idea that there'd be a whale of a story in it and that the publicity would do all three of us a lot of good. He was going to write the story and plant it with one of the national magazines. And before we left he did plant a few items about it in Lyons and Wilson and Kilgallen.* John and I began to get enthusiastic about it, too."

* Leonard Lyons, Earl Wilson, and Dorothy Kilgallen were all newspaper columnists.

"Why didn't you bring photographers along and do it for *Life?*" I asked.

"We were going to take pictures," he said. "It was Herman's idea that we would explore the area first. If we found the treasure, we'd go back and find it all over again for a photographer. If we didn't find any—well, Herman was going to buy a few old coins or something and bury them for us to find. He had it all worked out."

"Not quite all," I said dryly. "Of course, on the other hand, the way it has worked out, you'll probably get a lot more publicity than the other way."

He looked startled. "Oh, nothing like that," he said. "It wasn't in the plans. Besides, Herman was much too smart. Vanishing acts have been done too often."

"Especially the permanent kind," I pointed out. "Tell me something else. Why the life insurance policies?"

"That was Herman's idea, too. He said it would make the publicity even better by making the expedition look dangerous."

"Well, I guess Herman finally went too far with his stage setting," I said. "What did you do when you got here?"

"Herman was running things by that time," he said. "We knew that the map showed the treasure to be on Placide Island and there wasn't any reason why we couldn't have hired a boat and gone out to look. But Herman insisted on hiring a genuine Creole guide, and he was on cloud nine when he learned about the diviner. Said it would be terrific for the story. You know about the diviner?"

I nodded.

"So we hired Narcisse Coillon, the guide, and his diviner, Willie Morell. The diviner gave us a lot of advice about hunting for treasure, which Herman wrote down. It was pretty funny stuff. He also said we'd have to make the trip at night, as around there the spirits were the strongest in the daytime."

"Where can those two be reached?" I asked.

He thought for a minute and then gave me Coillon's address, which I wrote down. "We never had an address for Willie," he said. "Coillon got him for us."

"Okay. What did you do then?"

"Well, the day before we were supposed to make the trip, Coillon hired a boat to take us over that night. But when we showed up at the docks, it wasn't there. It never did come. Coillon kept trying to find an available boat without any luck. Then this other boat came in to dock and Herman decided that we had to hire it because it would be better for the pictures when we took them. Coillon tried to talk him into waiting until we could get a smaller boat, but there was no stopping Herman when he got his mind on something. So he went and talked to the guy who owned the boat and ended up by hiring him. A fellow named West Carroll. Supposed to be quite a skin diver and usually only takes out people who are interested in that sport. But Herman talked him into it."

"Know where he lives?"

"No."

"Okay," I said. "And when did you hire Eddie Capo?"

"Who?" he asked. There was a puzzled look on his face and I was pretty sure he wasn't that good an actor. "We only hired the three men. Didn't need any more."

"Forget it," I said. "Go ahead with the story."

"Well, we went to the island that night and the diviner went through a whole bunch of stuff and then started waving a forked stick over the ground. Herman had been fascinated up to then, but he started getting impatient. Finally, he said he and John would cut around the other way on the island and meet us somewhere on the other side. I don't know what the idea was, unless he wanted to spot picture possibilities."

"In the dark?"

"He and John both had powerful flashlights. I tried to get them to stay with us and Coillon warned them about quicksand, but Herman insisted. So off they went, while Coillon and I followed the diviner and his forked stick. It must have been about a half hour later when I heard one of the boys shout on the other side of the island. I couldn't tell which one it was, but he sounded pretty frightened. Coillon and I both shouted at them, but there was no answer. Finally, we ran around to the other side, but there was no sign of them. We got Carroll from the boat and we searched over the whole island, without finding a single trace of either of them. That's the story." He spread his hands.

"What do you think happened?" I asked.

"The only thing that could have," he said. "They must have stumbled into one of the quicksand pits that Coillon had warned them about. There probably wasn't time for more than that one shout. Poor devils."

"Why do you say the only thing that could have happened?" I asked.

"What else could have happened?" he asked.

The bartender arrived with two more drinks and I waited until he had retreated.

"There are several possibilities," I said. "The two of them could have slipped off the island in a rowboat without anyone being the wiser. They could have been kidnapped by someone and taken away in a rowboat. Or they could have been killed by someone."

"I suppose you mean me again," he said, his face darkening. "Why would I do anything like that?"

"You might have a hundred thousand reasons," I said. I waited a second before I went on. "But I didn't say you. I said somebody."

"I'm the only person Herman and John knew in New Orleans," he said.

"Believe it or not," I told him, "there are circles in which a proper introduction is not necessary in order to commit murder. No, Lane, if I become certain that you did it, I'll say so, not just hint at it. In fact, I admit that while I have no other candidates, I find it difficult to believe that you would kill anyone. Not because you wouldn't want to, but because it would hurt your chances of becoming a vice-president one of these days. And you, my boy, are vice-presidential timber if I ever saw any."

"What are you talking about?" he demanded.

"Just babbling," I told him. "I have an office on Madison Avenue and sometimes it rubs off on me. You know how it is, birds of a feather often get ruffled."

I was getting in over his head and I think he decided to ignore it on the grounds that I'd been drinking. "It had to be an accident," he said. "Nobody would kill John and Herman."

"It's just possible that somebody did," I pointed out. "But we'll see. Thanks for the talk. I'll see you around." I finished my drink and stood up.

"You probably will," he said gloomily. "The police say I can't leave yet. Let me know if you learn anything."

"Sure," I said. I looked around the bar. Another customer had joined us at the bar a few stools away. The redhead was still down at the other end of the bar. The newcomer was looking at her, too. I decided that Lane would probably move too slowly and maybe I ought to help him out. "Wait a minute," I said. I walked down to the end of the bar and sat on the stool next to the redhead.

"I'm a Boy Scout," I said solemnly, "the Eager Beaver Patrol, and I haven't done my good deed for today. So, first, I want to tell you that you're pretty. Very pretty." She thought about it a second, then decided she was safe in the hotel. She looked at me and smiled. "Thank you," she said. She was even nicer up close than at a distance. For a minute I thought of letting Lane shift for himself.

"Don't you think," I asked her, "that you and I would have met in Paris last summer—if we'd both been there?"

"I *was* in Paris last summer," she said.

"And I was in Rome—which is probably why we didn't meet in Paris. But it did make us practically neighbors. You've probably forgotten my name, but it's Milo March. I could never forget your face, but I'm afraid I have forgotten your name."

She smiled again. "It's Linda Ellen," she said.

"Of course," I said. "You know, I'm sorry I can't spend the afternoon in here, cutting up old touches with you. There must be something I can do to make it up to you. ... I have it. Come with me."

She let me take her hand and she followed meekly as I led her up to the other end of the bar where Peter Lane sat. He was pretending to be staring at his glass as if unaware that I'd been talking to her. He probably thought I was taking her off somewhere.

"My dear," I said to her, "I'd like to present a friend of mine, Mr. Peter Lane. He's a native of Madison Avenue in New York, so if he occasionally makes strange noises, they're merely some of his tribal chants. Otherwise, he's a fine specimen."

Lane got off the stool faster than anyone I ever saw. "Peter," I said gravely, "I'd like you to meet Miss Linda Ellen. I don't believe I have to mention that she's beautiful. Linda and I almost became very good friends in Paris last summer. Now, why don't you buy her a drink and pretend that I've gone— which I have." With that I turned and walked out, leaving them standing there. But I was sure they'd make out all right. I felt just like Elsa Maxwell, only slimmer.*

Upstairs, I decided I'd done about enough work for one day. It was getting too late to do very much, and I thought I might catch up on some of the sleep I'd lost the night before. But first I put in a long-distance call to Martin Raymond in New York.

"Milo, boy," he said, coming on the phone, "don't tell me you have it all solved already?"

---

* Elsa Maxwell was a gossip columnist and society hostess with a talent for match-making.

"All right, I won't," I said. "In fact, I couldn't without lying just a little. I've spent the day talking to the police and to Lane, and the case is slightly more complicated than it looked at first."

"How?"

"There are more angles to it," I said evasively. "But I called to say you'd better send me some more money just in case I need it."

"What?" he shouted. "We just gave you five hundred yesterday. What are you doing, buying the hotel?"

"No, just the gin at the hotel bar. I'm saving you money by having them leave most of the vermouth out. But tomorrow I'm going to hire the same three men that your policyholders did. I don't know how much everything will run, but send me three hundred more and I'll try to make it stretch."

"What will I tell the board?" he said.

"Tell them I love them and will think of them every time I spend a dollar," I said. "In the meantime, get the money off to me here at the hotel. If we talk any longer, you may have to send more to cover the phone bill. I am pinching pennies, you know. Good-bye." I put the receiver down before he could object further.

I had another small shot of Canadian Club. Then I picked up the phone and left a wake-up call. I stripped off my clothes and tumbled into bed. I was asleep almost as soon as my head hit the pillow.

The telephone brought me out of it. I groped for the receiver and answered. It was the operator telling me it was time to get up. I asked her to give me room service. When I got them

I told them to send me up a cup of coffee and some ice. I sat up on the edge of the bed and stayed there groggily until the boy arrived with the ice and coffee. By the time I'd finished the coffee, I was awake. By the time I'd finished my first drink and my second cigarette, I was ready to start moving.

I went into the bathroom and showered and shaved. I had another drink while I was dressing. Then I went downstairs, got a cab, and gave the driver Lisette's address.

She was ready when I got there, and she looked even more beautiful than she had in New York or on the plane.

"What would you like to see?" she asked as we came down the stairs from her apartment.

"You," I said.

"You are seeing me," she said with a smile. "Have you ever been in New Orleans before?"

"Yes, but I didn't see much of the town. I leave it up to you, honey. Wherever you go, you can be sure I'm following." I wasn't just making it up as I went along. She had me breathing like a schoolboy.

"Well," she said, "I guess we'll start with the one place every tourist should go. We'll have dinner at Antoine's."

"On to Antoine's," I said, hailing a cab.

"This time," she said as we entered the restaurant, "I'll decide what we should have. All right?"

"Okay," I said.

So we had two Sazerac cocktails apiece. I was going to have a third, but she said it would make the waiter unhappy because then he'd think I wouldn't appreciate the food. Not wanting to make any waiter unhappy, I gave up the idea.

It was worth it. First we had some Gulf shrimp, followed by Chicken Rochambeau, Soufflé Potatoes, a green salad, and a bottle of good wine. If I'd been with any woman other than the blonde, I would have probably ignored her completely. As it was, the food almost got the upper hand. Then we had crêpes Suzette, New Orleans coffee, and brandy.

"You like New Orleans coffee?" she asked.

"Love it," I said. "It's the only place where they make it 'black as hate, strong as love.' "

She looked at me and smiled. "You managed to pick up quite a bit of information in those bars," she said.

"I told you," I said. "I graduated cum laude. I'm now doing postgraduate work."

"Doctorate?" she asked.

"No. A degree in martinis."

We finished dinner and went out into the night. "We're on the town?" she asked.

"On the town," I agreed.

"Do you like jazz?"

"The most."

She laughed and led the way to a taxi. We took it over to Bourbon Street to the Paddock Bar and Lounge. We sat there, drinking and getting acquainted while we listened to a jazz band that sent the notes crawling up and down our spines.

We stayed there several hours and then went walking back up Bourbon Street, hand in hand, to the Café Laffite. We watched the place fill up with characters while we had a nightcap, a couple of repeats, and then a couple more for the road. If there's anything I can't stand it's a thirsty road.

It was about three o'clock when we finally reached her apartment. She stopped at the bottom of the stairs and looked at me. "Have fun?" she asked.

"The most," I said. "You?"

She nodded. "I did, Milo. Even more than I expected to. And now—good night."

"Aren't you even going to ask me up for a nightcap?" I asked.

She shook her head. "I have a feeling that you're the kind of man who would try to turn a nightcap into a nightgown."

"Well … ," I said. I had to admit she was right. "We could at least try and find out."

"Not tonight," she said. She reached out and touched my cheek with her hand. It was almost a caress.

"I'll see you tomorrow night?" I asked.

"If you'd like."

"I like."

"All right," she said. "Come at the same time. Good night, Milo."

"Good night," I said. I watched her walk up the stairs; then I went looking for a taxi.

It was after three-thirty when I got back to the hotel. I was feeling pretty good. I hummed a song to myself as I unlocked the door to my room and stepped inside. I closed the door and reached for the light switch.

"Please don't turn on the light, Mr. March," a voice said. "I don't care for too much light. And I very much fear that Eddie Capo is in a room across the street and he just might shoot if the light is turned on, even though I've told him not to."

FIVE

I stood for a minute with my hand on the switch, trying to make up my mind. If I'd already had that permit and the gun that went with it, I think I might have taken my chance. I was beginning to feel as if I were rooming in Grand Central Station, and I didn't like it. Finally I let my hand drop and looked around the room. My eyes had become accustomed to the darkness and I could make out a figure sitting in the upholstered chair that was near the foot of the bed.

"That was very intelligent of you, Mr. March," the voice said. "But then I expected you to act intelligently."

I walked over and sat on the bed. "Is it all right if I smoke a cigarette in my own room?" I asked. "Or will Eddie shoot the match out of my hand?"

"I doubt if even Eddie shoots that well," he said with a chuckle. "Of course you may smoke, Mr. March."

I got out a cigarette and lit it, hoping the match would light up the room enough so that I could see something of my visitor. But it didn't work. His hat was well down over his face and his coat collar was turned up. So all I knew about him came from his voice. From that I could guess that he was an old man. Maybe somewhere in his seventies, but well preserved.

"Who are you?" I asked.

"You may call me Eddie's employer for the moment," he said. "Perhaps one day we will meet in more revealing light, but for the moment I prefer to be anonymous."

"If you're his employer," I said, "I guess Eddie must have told you that I said you shouldn't send a boy to do a man's work."

"Eddie told me many things," he said, "including the fact that he wanted to come back and kill you. Of course I refused permission. But I have never seen Eddie quite so emotional, and I confess that it made me curious about the man who could cause his state of mind."

"So you came to visit me just to satisfy your curiosity?"

"Only partly so, Mr. March. My curiosity made me call certain friends of mine in New York to ask if they knew of you. It seems that they do. What they told me made me more curious. A man who is intelligent and learned, a man who appreciates the beautiful things in life, and at the same time a violent man. It is an unusual combination."

"Is it?" I asked. "If you dropped around to talk about Picasso's Blue Period, whether Marlowe wrote Shakespeare's works or not, or the philosophy of Camus, I'll be glad to oblige, but I would prefer a more convenient hour. Or should we, perhaps, talk about murder?"

"I'm sure that you could discuss all of those things, Mr. March," he said, "and I'm equally sure that I would enjoy the conversation. But I fear that was not why I came."

"Why did you?"

"Call it a quixotic desire to save a life."

"Whose?"

"Yours, Mr. March."

"Oh, we're going to do that bit again," I said wearily. "Everybody is suddenly worried about my health. First Eddie Capo, now you. Why?"

"I have known Eddie Capo for several years," he said, "and while he is a very efficient man in many respects, no one would ever accuse him of being overly intelligent. But for the first time in his life, Eddie is right in his thinking. You are a dangerous man, Mr. March. You may mix into things which do not concern you, and I would be forced to let Eddie have his wish about killing you."

"Why should that bother you?" I asked.

"I abhor violence, Mr. March. But I have been fated in my life to be associated with violent men. Many years ago, when I was a young man, I studied painting in Paris. I lived in a section that was frequented by the Apaches.* Now I am surrounded by men like Eddie Capo."

"Maybe you should get into another line of business," I suggested. "Something like flower arranging. I don't believe there are many violent men in that line."

He chuckled. "I daresay you're right, Mr. March. Unfortunately, I like money. I doubt if other lines of endeavor would recompense me as well as the one I'm now in."

"And what line is that?" I asked.

He chuckled again. "That, Mr. March, is exactly what I consider no concern of yours. If you were to return to New York immediately, you might be no wiser than when you came, but you would be ... alive."

---

* Les Apaches (which I assume this cultured man pronounces in the French manner) were a violent gang of Parisian street criminals.

"Let's get one thing straight," I said. "Why do you think I'm in New Orleans?"

"I know why you're here, Mr. March. It's about that unfortunate accident on Placide Island."

"Accident?"

"Accident," he repeated firmly.

"If it was an accident," I said, "I fail to see where it is any concern of yours or why you should care that I find out it was an accident."

He sighed heavily. "Mr. March, I will be honest with you, since you are an intelligent man. It was an accident. There was absolutely no need for anything to have happened to those two men. I assure you that I did not order it. However, it did occur and it is best for all concerned that nothing more happens."

"I don't agree," I said.

"I'm sorry, Mr. March. I'm really speaking for your own good."

"Why me?" I asked. "Even if I went back to New York, the police would still work on it."

"For a time," he said. "The police here are very efficient, but they work in certain ways which do not alarm me. I have reason to believe that you are quite different. Incidentally, Mr. March, you may be amused to know that you might not even have come to my attention—at least not at once—if it hadn't been for another accident."

"Accident?"

"Yes. I also did not order Eddie Capo to see you. He learned about your presence and took it upon himself to warn you.

It was an error on his part, but a fortunate one. His reaction to you made me curious enough to make inquiries. That, in turn, caused me to pay a visit, something which I seldom do."

"I'm flattered," I said.

"Of course," he said, as if it were to be taken for granted. "Mr. March, it seems to me that your insurance company can only be interested in finding out if the third man—Lane, isn't it?—had anything to do with what happened to his comrades. Your responsibility should end there. In the meantime, I assure you that Mr. Lane had nothing whatsoever to do with the accident."

"Great," I said. "I'm to go back and tell the company that we have the word of a man who comes in the dark and gives no name."

He sighed heavily. "I take it then, Mr. March, that you refuse to give up this futile search and return to New York?"

"Yeah," I said. "Now I'll make you an offer. You give the impression that you know exactly what happened to the two men. You say it was not something you ordered. Okay. You turn over to me whoever was responsible for it, with proof, and then I won't have to look any further. And I will go back to New York shortly thereafter."

"I'm sorry, Mr. March, but that is quite impossible. While it is true that someone acted without orders, there is an old Creole proverb here in New Orleans which says: *On préfère laver son linge sale en famille.* It means that we prefer to wash our dirty linen at home, not in public."

"I understood it," I said. "And the Creoles didn't invent it; they only translated it. Now, if you don't mind, it is late and I'm tired."

"Of course, Mr. March," he said. He stood up. "I'm sorry, sir, that you leave me no choice."

"Sure you are," I said. "One more thing. You seem to be fond of making a profit on everything. So if you're thinking of sending your pet monkey, Eddie Capo, after me, take out some insurance on him."

"I shall keep that in mind, sir," he said. He opened the door and was gone. There was nothing to see in the light from the corridor but the hat and the bulky overcoat.

I walked over to the window and looked out. My room fronted on the street. Across from me there was a building that looked like an apartment house. All the windows were dark, but a minute later I saw the red glow of a cigarette through the window directly opposite me. I watched. Whoever was smoking got up and moved across the room. The glow was still for a couple of minutes, then moved back across the room and vanished.

I had a hunch about it. I switched my gaze down to the front door of the building. In a little bit Eddie Capo came out of the door. He went down the street and got into a big black Cadillac. The car made a U-turn in the street and then I couldn't see it, but I had an idea it had stopped momentarily in front of the hotel. I went over and picked up the receiver on the phone.

"Let me have the desk," I told the sleepy operator.

It must have taken three or four rings before the man at the desk answered.

"This is Milo March in three seventeen," I told him. "A man just left the hotel. I'd like to know who he was."

"I'm sorry, sir," the clerk said, "but I didn't see anyone leave."

I hung up and cursed. I would have believed he was lying, but he'd sounded as if he'd been asleep when my call came in. I went over and turned on the light. It was four-thirty in the morning. I stripped off my clothes and tumbled into bed. I'd worry about the situation after I had some sleep.

It was nine o'clock when I awakened the next morning. The way I felt, all I wanted to do was turn over and go back to sleep, but I knew I'd have to do better than that if I wanted to earn my hundred a day. I called downstairs for a pot of coffee and took a quick shower while I was waiting for it.

Three cups of coffee, three cigarettes, and one drink of whiskey later, I was ready to face the world. I got dressed and went downstairs. There was a Western Union order for three hundred dollars from Intercontinental and a telegram from Johnny Rockland waiting for me. I cashed the money order at the desk and read the telegram while I was having breakfast in the coffee shop.

NAME OF THE MAN YOU'RE INTERESTED IN NOT KNOWN TO OUR PIGEONS HERE. KNOWN ONLY AS THE PAINTER. NEVER ATTENDS SYNDICATE MEETINGS UP HERE. SAID TO BE ONE OF THE TOP FOUR. LUCK.

JOHNNY ROCKLAND

I walked out of the hotel and looked up at the third floor of the building across the street. There was an empty look about the windows. I walked across the street and entered the building. I rang the bell under the sign that said *Supt.* After a couple of minutes the door opened and a woman, in a wrapper and with her hair up in curlers, looked out.

"Yes?" she asked.

"Is the front apartment on the third floor for rent?" I asked.

"You're a day late," she said. "It was just rented yesterday. And it was the last vacancy I had."

"That's too bad," I said. "Would you mind telling me who rented it?"

"A Mr. Edward Capo," she said.

I thanked her and left, taking a taxi down to Police Headquarters. Lieutenant Stern had the gun permit ready for me. I was fingerprinted and mugged and then he gave it to me. I went to the shop he told me about and bought a short-barreled .32 and a shoulder holster. I walked back to Lieutenant Stern's office and they made a record of the serial number. I buckled on the holster, put the gun away, and was ready for business. Just feeling the gun under my arm made me more cheerful about the future.

"Just be careful who you shoot with it," the Lieutenant said.

"I'm always careful who I shoot," I told him. I debated with myself and decided not to tell him about my visitor of the night before. "I'll see you around, Lieutenant."

"I'll be around," he said.

I went out and got into a taxi, giving the driver the address of Narcisse Coillon that Peter Lane had given me. It turned out to be below Canal Street in the old Creole section. It was a tiny house, old but looking neat and well cared-for. I went up and knocked on the door. It opened and a man looked out. He was tall and stooped, with powerful shoulders. My guess was that he was probably about fifty, but his hair was still black. He had a sharp and proud face.

"Narcisse Coillon?" I asked.

"Yes," he said.

"My name is Milo March," I said. "I would like to talk to you."

"Come in," he said. He stepped aside and I entered the house. He led the way into a living room that was just as neat as the outside. The furniture all looked as if it had been around for a century. "I was just having coffee," he said. "Will you join me?"

"With pleasure," I said.

He left the room, soon returning with a cup of the familiar black coffee. I took the cup and thanked him.

"I am looking for a guide," I said, "and I was told that you were the best."

He accepted the compliment as his due. "May I ask who recommended me?"

"Peter Lane," I said.

Something crossed his face, no more than a shadow. "I am honored that Mr. Lane recommends me. His trip was a most unfortunate one."

"I know," I said. "I'll be honest with you, Mr. Coillon. I am from New York. I am here especially to look into what happened to Mr. Lane's two companions. I shall want to talk to you about that. But I also want to hire you for at least one trip. And I'd like to hire the same diviner Mr. Lane used, if you'll tell me how to contact him."

"I can hire him for you. I expect him to be here within a few minutes if you'd like to meet him first. Are you also searching for pirate treasure, Mr. March?" There was something like contempt just beneath the surface of his words.

"In a way," I said.

"Do you also have a map?"

"No map."

"Where do you want to go?" he asked.

"Placide Island," I said.

The shadow crossed his face again. "You are looking for the same treasure Mr.

Lane was after?"

"No," I said. "I'm looking for a different treasure."

"If you are interested in buried treasure," he said, "there are many spots. Old coins have even been found at the corner of Orleans and Bourbon streets. Then there are the Isle de Gombi, Grand Isle where Laffite had his headquarters, several places in Jefferson Parish—"

"I like Placide Island best," I said. "I have feelings about things like that. Now, about the other matter—I understand that you believe the two men met with an accident?"

"What else could have happened to them?" he asked. "There are many very dangerous pits of quicksand on that island. I warned them, but it would still be easy for a stranger to get caught in the quicksand before he knew what was happening."

"What about the bodies?"

"Ah," he said. He spread his hands. "No one knows how far down the quicksand goes. It is doubtful if one could ever find a body in one of those pits."

"And you think that is the only possibility?"

"What else? The two men were strangers here. Who would wish them harm?"

"Who indeed?" I said. "Were you with Mr. Lane all the time you were on the island?"

"Yes."

"Do you know Eddie Capo well?" I asked.

"Capo—that was not the name of either of the other two men, was it?" he asked politely. "I'm afraid that it is not a familiar name to me."

It was impossible for me to tell whether he was lying or not.

"When did you wish to go to Placide Island?" he asked.

"I think tomorrow night," I said. "I still have to arrange for a boat to take us, but would that be all right with you?"

"I believe so."

"Just to make certain that you can make it," I said, "I am willing to hire you today and pay you for today and tomorrow both. What do you charge per day?"

"I get thirty-five," he said, "and the diviner gets twenty dollars."

"That will be fine," I told him. I took out some money and counted out seventy dollars. "Here is two days in advance for you."

He took the money and placed it in his pocket. There was a knock on the door.

"That's probably Willie now," he said. He got up and left the room.

When he came back there was a husky young Negro with him. He looked to be in his early twenties, with a very black face, the white teeth exposed in a grin that seemed to be permanent. He held his hat in his hand, and his head was bent forward as though to indicate a perpetual bow.

"This is Willie," Coillon said. "Willie, this is Mr. March. He wants to hire a diviner for tomorrow night. To go to Placide Island."

"Yes, sir," Willie said. His smile stayed the same and there was no way to tell how he felt about going back to the island.

"How are you, Willie?" I said.

"I feels so feelsy, sir," he said. His voice was rich and thick, like those of many Southern Negroes, so that his words sounded as if they were coming through molasses.

"Willie is one of the best diviners and spirit controllers in the state," Coillon said. "He's lazy, so he only works part of the year, but he's good."

"All right, Willie," I said. "I'm hiring you for today and tomorrow, and we'll go out tomorrow night. I'll pay you now for the two days." I counted out forty dollars and handed it to him. "Is that right?"

"Yes, sir," he said, bobbing his head. He put the money in his pocket without looking at it.

"You think we might find any treasure, Willie?" I asked curiously.

"If it's there, I finds it," he said. "But I don't do no diggin'. I just finds the treasure and fights the spirits. There ain't none of them can mess with me."

"What kind of spirits?" I asked.

"They is land spirits and water spirits. They is seven kind of land spirits and that makes trouble. There is bulls, lions, dogs, babies, snakes, people, and pearls. If'n you sees a cat, that's bad. You gotta be careful and you gotta be clean. You sure can't touch no woman, not even your wife, for four days before you starts out."

"That finishes me as a spirit controller," I said. "How do you go about finding the treasure, Willie?"

"I uses my divining stick to tell me where it is. When I finds it, I drives sticks in a circle and ties clothesline to them. It's gotta be thirteen feet to the north, thirteen feet to the east, thirteen feet to the south, thirteen feet to the west. You gets inside the ring and there ain't nobody can talk or sweat or spit. That brings the bad spirits. Then I reads the Twenty-first Psalm and somebody starts diggin'."

"Sounds real jazzy," I said. "Willie, I have a feeling you should take that bit up to New York. You'd make a fortune on Madison Avenue keeping bad spirits away from the advertising copy. Of course, you'd have to learn to drink very dry martinis."

"Yes, sir," he said. "Sometimes a little liquor is good. Some spirits like to get drunk. But there is lots of things you gotta watch or the bad spirits move in. Can't take no lemon anyways, or maybe you has a big snake standing right over you."

"Yeah," I said. "Well, unless I get in touch with you to change it, meet me at the dock tomorrow night about nine o'clock."

"All right, we'll be there," Coillon said.

I went out and walked up the street until I found a taxi to take me to the dock. I got out at the end of the street and walked out on the pier. Obviously quite a number of boats had already gone out, but there were still many there, looking sleek and trim as they bobbed with the movement of the water. There were quite a few people on the pier who were certainly tourists, either waiting to go out on a boat or just looking.

I walked along until I came to a boat with a man on the deck. I stopped and waited until he looked up. "Can you tell me where to find West Carroll?"

He turned his head to look down the line of boats. "He's still in," he said. "Six boats down. The *Mary Anne*."

"Thanks," I said. I went on down to the *Mary Anne*. She was a large white cruiser, well cared-for. A man was standing on the deck, polishing the brass on the running lights. He had enormous shoulders and powerful arms. He looked to be about thirty, with a strong, handsome face and curly brown hair. He probably was a tough man in a fight.

"I'm looking for West Carroll," I said, stopping by the prow.

He turned and looked me over lazily before answering. "Well, you've found him." He went back to polishing the brass.

"I want to hire your boat," I said.

"Skin diving?" he asked.

"No. I want to hire you for tomorrow night. About nine o'clock."

"I don't know," he said. "I'm busy later."

"I won't need you for more than about an hour. We'll be through by ten or ten-thirty," I assured him.

He looked around again. "Where do you want to go?"

"Placide Island," I said.

His face darkened. "What is this? A gag? Or are you another cop?"

"Neither," I said. "My name is Milo March. I'm from the insurance company that had policies on the two men who vanished two weeks ago on Placide Island. I want to go see the island. I've hired Coillon and Willie Morell to go along."

"Why pick on me?" he asked. "There are a lot of boats for hire."

"I also want to talk to you. In the meantime, why not throw the business your way? Will you take me?"

"All right," he said. "But I have to be back here by ten-thirty. If you're not ready to leave, I'll come back without you."

"Fair enough," I said. I lit a cigarette and continued to stand there without saying anything. He finished with the one light and moved over to the other.

"What do you want to talk about?" he asked finally.

"What do you think happened to the two men?" I asked.

"Quicksand."

"No other possibility?"

"You talk like the cops," he said. "How the hell do I know? But it figures the guys don't know anybody here, so why is anybody going to kill them? Besides, there weren't any other boats running out there that night. I would've heard them."

"What about a rowboat?"

"That's possible," he admitted. "But who would do it?"

"Maybe Eddie Capo," I said.

"Who?"

"Eddie Capo."

"Who's he?"

"Forget it," I said. "You heard the shout that night?"

"Yeah. I was on the boat waiting for them and I heard it."

"Was it one man or two who shouted?"

"Sounded like one."

"What did you do?"

"Nothing."

"Why not?"

"How the hell did I know anything was wrong?" he said. "I thought maybe the guy found a bottle cap and believed he'd found a Spanish doubloon."

"It sounded like that kind of shout?"

He shrugged. "It was just a shout. I didn't try to figure out what kind. I never thought anybody would get into trouble on Placide Island."

"But they did," I pointed out.

"Only because they didn't stay with Coillon," he said. "He knows all the quicksand pits and they would've been all right if they hadn't insisted on going off by themselves."

"Okay," I said. "I'll see you here tomorrow night at nine."

"I'll be here," he said.

I turned and went back the way I'd come, thinking about the case. The more I heard the quicksand solution, the less I liked it—and that wasn't only because of Eddie Capo and his bashful boss. But I still didn't know where to start, except to keep going over and over the stories until something turned up. Then I got a break even though it took a few minutes for me to realize that's what it was.

I reached the end of the pier and stopped to see if I could

spot a taxi anywhere. There wasn't one in sight. I debated with myself whether to wait or walk a couple of blocks where I might have a better chance. Two women were walking toward me, obviously dressed to go out fishing.

"… and he's so handsome," one of the women was saying. "My dear, wait until you see him. I'm so glad that George couldn't go fishing today."

The other woman said something that I didn't hear. "Oh, you'll love it," the first one said. "Wait until we take you out tonight and show you some of the places we've discovered. You just wouldn't believe it."

The second woman murmured something else. "Everything is fantastic in New Orleans," the first woman said. "You should have gotten here yesterday. We were taken through a house that was once a very fancy—you know—brothel. Maybe George will take us there again so you can see it. And the other day I saw something you simply wouldn't believe. It was a week ago—no, two weeks ago yesterday—when George made me get up and go fishing with him at six o'clock in the morning. My dear, it was ghastly. Then just as we got here, there was a hearse pulling away from the dock. But it was a bright red hearse. Imagine."

SIX

Having decided that it would be better to walk to where I could get a cab and having already started, I never did hear the other woman's reaction to a red hearse. The idea of a red hearse amused me and I was smiling to myself as I walked along. I had gone a block before I realized that she had said something else that interested me even more. She had said she saw the red hearse leaving the dock at six o'clock in the morning. And the day she had mentioned had been the morning after the disappearance of the two men.

I brooded about this while I took a taxi back to the hotel. I went into the dining room and had my usual two martinis and then lunch. After lunch I hunted up a public phone booth and put in a call to Lieutenant Stern.

"Got it all worked out?" he said when he came on the phone.

"Just listening to the testimony," I said. "I called you about something else. You know anything about an undertaker in New Orleans who drives a red hearse?"

"Yeah, there is a guy," he said, "but I don't remember his name. The red hearse has been around a long time, practically a landmark. He does a big business among some of the Negro families who don't like to have their funerals too dreary. Why?"

"Somebody told me about it," I said, "and I thought I was being kidded. You're the only native I knew to check it with."

"Stay around a few days and you'll probably see it," he said. "I've seen it around on the streets for so many years I guess I'd almost forgotten it is red. Seen any more of your friend, Eddie Capo?"

"No, but he'll probably be around one of these days. I'll ship the body to you."

"You do that," he said.

"Okay, thanks, Lieutenant. I'll be talking to you." I hung up and went into the bar for a quiet drink. I thought maybe I'd see Peter Lane in there, but there was no sign of him. Maybe the redhead had been too much for him.

I had a drink and asked the bartender about the red hearse. He remembered having seen it, but didn't have any idea who it belonged to. After I finished my drink I went upstairs to my room. I got out the classified phone directory and went to work. I started calling undertakers and asking them if they knew the man who had a red hearse. I made it on my fifth call.

"That's Adam Perrin," the man said. "You'll find him over on Perdido Street. Been using that red hearse for years. Once some church group wanted to make him stop, but there wasn't any law against it, so Adam's still driving it."

"Thanks," I said and hung up. I looked up Adam Perrin and found the address. Then I went back downstairs and took a taxi over to Perdido Street. When we got to the address, the red hearse was sitting out front. It was a bright red, too.

I paid off the driver and went in. There was a waiting room, filled with potted plants, the walls covered with various little mottoes concocted with the view of cheering up the relatives of the deceased. The waiting room smelled strongly of formaldehyde and embalming fluid. There was no one in the room, so I coughed and waited.

In a few minutes the back door opened and a man came out struggling into his coat. He straightened up as he saw me and came forward, his hands clasped in front of him.

"Good afternoon, sir," he said. His voice was smoothly melancholy as though with years of practice. "May I help you?"

"Maybe," I said. "I'm looking for Adam Perrin."

"I am Adam Perrin."

I took a good look at him. He was about forty-five years old and his hair had already receded some two inches from its original vantage point. He was tall, almost as tall as I am, but thin so that he probably didn't weigh more than one fifty or sixty. He wore a black suit, a white shirt, and a black shoestring tie. His face was the color of bread dough that has set out in the air too long.

"I can provide almost any sort of service you would like," he said. "We start with the deluxe service which includes a jazz band to follow the hearse—no, I guess you wouldn't want that. Let me see. Suppose we start with the simplest item. What sort of coffin did you have in mind?"

"I didn't have any coffin in mind," I said.

"Oh, my dear sir," he said, sounding shocked. "You must have a coffin. I believe it's even a city law. In twenty years I've never heard of anyone not having a coffin."

"Well, you've heard of it now," I said. "I've never had a coffin in my life."

"But you're alive," he said.

"I'm glad you noticed," I told him. "I think you misunderstand, Mr. Perrin. I'm not here to arrange a funeral."

"No?" he said. Something in his face changed. It lost its melancholy cast ever so subtly and the lines hardened. "Then why are you here?"

"For information."

"About funerals?"

"In a way," I said. "That red hearse you have out front. Is that the only one in the city?"

"The only one in the state," he said proudly. "If you know someone who wants to have a different kind of funeral, to get away from dull, conventional black, you've come to the right place."

"I don't know anyone who wants to have a funeral," I said, "although I've become acquainted with a few who may need one. But that's not the kind of information I want."

"What is it, then?" he asked harshly.

"Two weeks ago yesterday morning, at six o'clock," I said, "your red hearse was seen leaving the docks, where the fishing boats are moored."

"So?" he said. "Almost every day my red hearse can be seen in various parts of New Orleans. What of it?"

"What were you doing there?"

He stared at me for a minute. "I don't know that it is any of your business, but I was not at the dock. I had made a call down the street from the dock. Two brothers had died and I was asked to prepare them for burial."

"Isn't that hour of the morning rather unusual?"

"I don't see that it is. I had been requested to do it the night before, but was unable to go then. So I went early in the morning."

"Where down the street?" I asked. "What address?"

"Do you have a right to ask?" he wanted to know.

"If I don't," I said, "I'll go get a policeman who does have the right. What address?"

"Forty-seven."

"What was the brothers' name?"

"Anderson."

"And you arranged the funeral for the family?"

He nodded.

"Where did you bury them?"

"Girod Cemetery."

"And that's the whole story?" I asked.

"What do you expect?" he demanded. "I was hired to prepare the bodies and bury them. I did. I was paid for it. Sometimes I do this several times a day. That's the story. When Adam Perrin buries them, they stay buried; they do not get up and walk around New Orleans. And what right do you have to come around asking questions and hinting there is something wrong? I have been here for twenty years—me, Adam Perrin—and I have a good reputation as an undertaker." He had worked himself up to a rage by the time he finished.

"Okay, Adam," I said. "Sorry to have bothered you. Maybe I'll send you some business one of these days." I turned and started out.

"Who did you say you were?" he called after me.

"I didn't say," I told him and went on out. I found a cab and directed the driver back to the docks. There I walked down the street until I came to 47. It was a small, sagging house and didn't look as if it had been lived in for years. I went in through the gate and across the grass and weeds to the front door. I knocked loudly. There was no answer. I went over and looked in through the window. The house was empty and it looked as if the dust were inches thick.

I went back and took another cab down to police headquarters. It was time to bring in the reserves.

"What's the matter?" Lieutenant Stern asked as I came in. "Need some instructions in how to use the gun now that you have it?"

"Having done part of your work," I said, "I decided maybe I ought to let you finish it. Otherwise the taxpayers might get annoyed."

"Yeah?"

"Remember me asking you about the red hearse?"

"Yeah," he said. "I didn't think it was the casual question you pretended, but I couldn't see what it had to do with us."

"Well, it belongs to a man named Adam Perrin. He has a funeral parlor down on Perdido Street. Two weeks ago yesterday morning—which was the morning after our two men vanished—his red hearse was seen down by the docks. At six in the morning."

"Who saw it?"

"Some woman. A tourist. I just happened to hear her telling another woman about seeing a red hearse there that morning. It wasn't until I'd walked about a block that I realized what the day was."

"Some woman," he said. "What kind of witness is that?"

"But Perrin admitted he was down there that morning."

"You talked to him?"

"Yeah. He claims he wasn't at the dock. Says he was supposed to pick up the bodies of two brothers named Anderson who lived up the street from the dock. Says he picked them up there and then buried them in Girod Cemetery."

"What's wrong with that?"

"Just one thing. I pinned him down as to where he picked them up. He gave me the address. Forty-seven. I just came from there. Nobody lives at that address and I'd guess nobody has for many years."

"That's a little different," he said slowly.

"I'll make you a small bet," I told him. "You go out and dig up the Anderson brothers and I bet they turn out to be Herman Mack and John Bryant."

"If you're right about what you're saying, it might be a good bet," he said. "Okay, Milo, you've done your share of this; I'll take over. Want me to call you at your hotel?"

"You'd better," I said.

"As soon as we find out," he said. He got up and came around the desk. "Good work, Milo. I'm glad to see, too, that you know when to stop and didn't start out to dig up graves."

"Me?" I said. "I can't stand shovels. They put blisters on my hands. I stop when I've done the brainwork."

"Well, don't overdo it," he said dryly. "I'd hate to have to explain to New York why you suddenly collapsed. I'll call you."

I went out while he swung into action on the phone. It was

well past the middle of the afternoon and I decided I had put in a day's work and deserved a little relaxation. I went back to the hotel and started relaxing in the bar with some Canadian Club.

The bar was beginning to fill up, but Lane wasn't there. Neither was the redhead.

There was still no call for me when it was time to go upstairs and get ready for my date. So when I got to my room I put in a call to Stern. I half expected that he wouldn't be there, since he'd said he was on the early shift this week and it must have been about time for him to go home when I'd seen him. But he answered the phone.

"Thought you were going to call," I said.

"No identification yet," he said. "We've been trying to get hold of Lane for more than two hours to come look at them."

"I think he's been drowning his sorrow in redheads."

"Well, if we don't get him pretty soon, I'm going to put out a wanted call on him."

"Did you leave a message here for him?"

"Several of them."

"I have to go out," I said, "but I'll call in later. Who do I ask for if you're gone?"

"Sergeant Leroux."

"Okay. In the meantime, what do you think?"

"I think it's them," he said. "We found two men buried together and they look like the descriptions of Mack and Bryant. And they hadn't died natural deaths."

"How?"

"Knife. A big one, too, and used by somebody who knew

how to use it. If it's them, it's a wonder one of them even got that one yell out. They didn't have much time."

"What about the undertaker?"

"We brought him in and questioned him. We just let him go home a few minutes ago. I don't know, but he may be telling the truth. He claims he did get the bodies at that address. Of course, he realized that something was wrong. He saw they'd been knifed and he knew that nobody lived there as soon as he saw the house. At the best, he's guilty of withholding information and not reporting a crime. He says he got the order for the funeral by telephone and that the money was slipped under his door sometime that night. That's why he didn't go until early that morning. He wasn't going until he was paid. He still had the envelope the money came in, with his name cut out of one of his newspaper ads and pasted on it."

"He could have fixed that himself."

"Yeah, he could. He says they paid him enough to put up a headstone, too, with the name Anderson on it. He ordered and paid for the stone and it was put up two days ago. Doesn't hardly seem he'd do that if he were guilty, especially since he probably had no idea that he'd get tripped up."

"Not if it was just him," I admitted. "But if there was an organization involved, they might be that careful."

"That's true," he said. "Well, we could charge Perrin with not reporting a crime and withholding information, but it's not a very stiff charge. I think maybe it's better to let him go and sort of keep an eye on him. It won't be too hard; he even uses that red hearse for his personal trips."

"I guess you're right," I said. "Well, I'll call you later."

"Okay. I may not be here. I'm off for home the minute we get Lane. It's been a long day."

"Happy pipe and slippers," I told him and hung up. I went in and shaved and showered. By the time I was dressed I had only fifteen minutes to get to Lisette's.

I made it. We went over to Pat O'Brien's bar on St. Peter Street, where we had several drinks. Then from there we went to Arnaud's on Bienville and had a couple more drinks, followed by Shrimp Arnaud, trout meunière, Brabant potatoes, and a mixed green salad. After that, cherries jubilee and New Orleans coffee. Then we went uptown to the Blue Room at the Roosevelt Hotel, where we danced for several hours. Then back downtown to the Famous Door, not far from the Court of Two Sisters, to listen to more jazz.

We reached the stairway to Lisette's apartment at about two-thirty in the morning.

"It was even more fun than last night," she said. "Would you like to come up for a nightcap? I have some very nice brandy."

"I love brandy," I said gravely and followed her up the stairs.

The next morning I had my coffee in the Morning Call over in the old French Market section. When I got back to the hotel, I called Lieutenant Stern.

"Well, we finally got him this morning," he said. "He left here only a few minutes ago. You hit the jackpot, Milo."

"It's Mack and Bryant?"

"Yeah. Lane identified them. So now we know at least that they were murdered. Now the question is who."

"What about Perrin?"

"I'm going to talk to him again, but I think he was just used."

"I would suspect my own grandmother, if I had one, in this case," I said. "What's your next step?"

"Another talk with West Carroll, just in case he heard something else that night and forgot about it. And we'll start checking up as much as we can on small boats, particularly those that have outboard motors but that can also be rowed. We might stumble onto something. You know that police work is mostly just hard work and more hard work."

"Yeah."

"What are you going to do?" he asked.

"Just mess around in my usual fashion," I said. "Maybe it'll push Eddie Capo into doing something and then we might start to get somewhere. You see, I work from the other side of the fence. Sometimes if I push enough, somebody gets off balance and makes a mistake."

"Well, just be sure you don't push Eddie Capo into killing you."

"I don't think I'd care for that," I admitted.

"I still think I ought to pull him in and work him over as to why he threatened you."

"No," I said. "Nobody's made Eddie Capo talk in twenty years, so I don't think you'll succeed. In the meantime, if you don't pull him in, he'll think I didn't report it and it might make him a little bolder."

"Okay," he said wearily. "I know you're right about him talking or I wouldn't pay any attention to you. Want me to give you a police guard?"

"Hell, no," I said. "And if you try to stick one on me, I'll lose him fast. I'll keep in touch." I hung up and went to see if the bar was open. It was. If I was going to keep on without any more sleep than I'd been getting, I was going to need a little stimulant.

I was the first customer. I ordered a Canadian Club and water and sat nursing it. I really wanted to think about Lisette, who was beginning to grow on me, but I put her out of my mind. It was hard, for her perfume still clung to me. But I had to think about the case. I began to review it in my mind.

We now knew that the two men had been murdered. Peter Lane certainly had not done it directly, and I was beginning to feel that he hadn't had anything to do with it. His participation was the only thing that the insurance company would really be interested in, but the only way I could clear him was by proving who had done it. We knew, according to West Carroll, the boatman, that there hadn't been any other motorboats near the island at the time. Of course, he might be lying, but somebody might have gone part of the way by outboard motor and then rowed the rest of the way. But why? If the two men hadn't strayed away from Lane, the guide, and the diviner, probably nothing would have happened since nothing did happen to the three who were together. So why the other two?

Nothing made much sense. If the two men had stumbled onto an actual pirate treasure, someone might have killed them for it, but that would mean that the someone just happened to be hanging around a desolate island at the right time. Or knew the treasure was there and was watching to see that no one got it. I found both of those ideas hard to buy. But what did it leave?

It seemed unlikely that the two men were mixed up in anything serious enough to get them murdered. Probably their greatest crime was cheating on their wives. So maybe they had stumbled onto something on the island that was being watched. But what? Especially when the police and everyone claimed that nothing could possibly be hidden on that particular island.

On the other hand, there was Eddie Capo. And his mysterious boss. According to Johnny Rockland, the boss was probably somebody important in the Syndicate, the man known only as "The Painter." My visitor that night had mentioned that he studied painting in Paris when he was a young man. And Eddie Capo had worked for the Syndicate most of his adult life. So what was the relationship between the Syndicate and a publicity man and market research man? It just didn't make sense. Yet it had to, because Eddie and his boss were so anxious to keep me from solving the case. The man who visited me had said it was an accident, but all he seemed to have meant by that was that it wouldn't have been necessary to do anything to the two men. Could the two men have known something about the Syndicate operation without being aware that they knew? And that was why it was an accident?

And what was the Syndicate operation in New Orleans? From what Stern had said and what I already knew, their main operation was probably drugs. But again that brought up the fact that I couldn't see any connection between the two men and drugs.

Also, what about Adam Perrin, the undertaker with the red hearse? I wasn't so sure that he wasn't more involved than his story indicated. The problem was to try to fit all these people together.

"Oh, hello there," a voice said.

I looked up. It was Peter Lane. He looked drawn, as though the identification had been rough on him. It probably had. He ordered a double shot of whiskey.

"Well, they found them," he said dully.

"I know," I told him. "I also know that you just came from identifying them. It must've been rough."

"God, it was," he said. "They had been my friends since we were in school together. Why the hell would anyone kill them?"

"That's what we have to find out," I said. "How come it took the cops so long to locate you?"

He looked at me, thinking. Then, just for a moment, his face lost some of its gloom. "That friend of yours you introduced me to," he said. "That's a lot of woman." His face darkened again. "I don't suppose I should have done it under the circumstances, but I think maybe it kept me from flipping my wig. I was just about to, just hanging around here waiting for information."

"I understand," I told him. "Do you feel up to answering some more questions for me?"

"If I can," he said. "I'll do anything that will help to get whoever did this."

"Good boy," I said. "How long were the three of you here in New Orleans before you went to the island?"

"About a week, I guess. ... No, eight days, to be exact."

"What did you do during that time?"

"Do? Nothing very sensational. We spent part of the time trying to dig up information about Placide Island and in locating a good guide. Herman, of course, did a lot of skull work, figuring out new angles for the story."

"What else?"

"The usual thing, I guess. We went down to the French Quarter almost every night. Saw most of the girlie shows and heard a lot of jazz. We lapped up a lot of booze and I guess four or five nights we picked up some girls. You know how it is."

"I know how it is," I said, "but that's not really what I want. Think hard. Did anything unusual happen during those eight days?"

"Well, it wasn't like doing the clubs on the East Side of New York, but what do you mean by unusual?"

"Is there any chance that they stumbled onto something—maybe having to do with narcotics—without really being aware of its importance?"

"I don't think so," he said. "All we did was hit the regular tourist traps. We had a lot of fun, but nothing happened that I know about."

"How about the research on the island? Was there maybe anything strange or unusual in it?"

"It was just the usual stuff. Legends about pirates burying their treasure there and stories about people who had looked for it without finding it. There wasn't anything else that I saw."

"All right, another thing," I said. "You knew both of these guys for a long time, but forget for the moment that they were your friends. Is it possible that either one of them, or both, might have been mixed up in anything criminal? Now or in the past?"

He looked shocked. "Impossible. I'd stake my life on it. The nearest either of them ever came to breaking the law was getting a parking ticket or maybe going to a bottle club. Nothing else."

"Could either one of them have used drugs?"

"Absolutely not. Why all these questions about drugs?"

"Just questions," I said. "The night you went to the island, what time did you get there?"

"It must have been about eleven. We were more than an hour late."

"Why?"

"Well, the boatman Coillon had hired for us never showed up. He tried to line up another but they were either not available or didn't want to work that late. Then about ten-thirty this fellow Carroll came into the dock and we got him to take us."

Well, that complicated it even more, as if I needed it. If their schedule was off an hour, it made it even more difficult to see the plan by which they were killed.

"Did you have any idea earlier," I asked, "that Bryant and Mack were going off alone on the island?"

"No. They decided suddenly."

"Did Coillon, the guide, do anything about encouraging them to go off alone?"

"Quite the contrary. He joined me in doing everything possible to get them to stay with us. Even after they had started off, I remember he shouted after them to urge them to reconsider and to warn them again about the quicksand."

"What about the diviner?"

"He didn't do anything except to say that there were lots of bad spirits on the island."

"Okay," I said wearily. I was getting nowhere. I decided that I'd go upstairs and take a short nap. Maybe then I could start fresh. "I'll talk to you again."

"All right," he said. He was staring moodily at his drink as I left the bar.

I took the elevator upstairs and started for my room at the front of the corridor. I'd gone only a few steps when I saw the door to my room open and a man come out. He bent down, carefully locking the door again. Then he turned to leave.

It was Eddie Capo.

SEVEN

He didn't see me at first. He started to walk toward the elevators, with his head down. Then he looked up and saw me. He stopped, his legs slightly spraddled, a watchful look on his face.

"You should have told me that you were coming to visit," I said. I kept walking carefully toward him. "I would have stayed home and made tea for you."

He didn't say anything, but just stood there and watched me. His right hand wasn't far from the lapel of his coat

"Were you looking for something, Eddie?" I asked. I stopped a couple of feet away from him.

"Go to hell, snooper," he said.

"Ah, but you're mixed up, Eddie," I told him. "It was you who were snooping. I haven't quite made up my mind yet, but I don't think I like it."

"No?" he said. That eager look was back in his eyes again. "What are you going to do about it?"

"Not much," I said. "Just this—" I hit him as hard as I could in the mouth. He went back, caromed off the wall, and stumbled to the floor. I moved in fast and kicked as he reached with his right hand for the gun under his left arm. The gun clanged off the wall and spun on the floor. I went over and picked it up, dropping it in my pocket. Then I looked at Eddie.

He was getting up from the floor. There was a thin trickle of blood running from the corner of his mouth. The eagerness in his eyes was a hunger now as he looked at me.

"Want more, Eddie?" I asked.

"Give me my gun," he said. His voice was no more than a whisper.

I took his gun from my pocket and broke it open. I took out the shells and tossed him the empty gun. He caught it with his right hand, and his left hand went into his pocket. It came out full of shells. He snapped the gun open and started to feed them in.

I stepped in fast and hit him again. He went down, the bullets flying over the floor. He got up on his hands and knees and reached for a bullet on the floor. I kicked his hand aside. There wasn't a sound from him as he looked up at me, but his face was contorted with pain and a kind of madness.

"I don't mind killing you, Eddie," I said, "but I'm not ready yet, so don't push it."

He called me a name, one that you won't find in the family dictionary.

"Get up and get out," I said. "Now. Go back and tell your boss, who's afraid to show his face, to keep you off my back or the next time I will hurt you."

He slowly got up from the floor and stood, gun dangling from his hand, staring at me as though he were trying to memorize every line in my face. Then he turned and walked down the stairs next to the bank of elevators.

I waited, listening to his footsteps going down the stairs until they finally faded out. Then I turned and went into my room. He'd gone through everything pretty thoroughly and hadn't made any attempt to make it look as if the room hadn't been searched. I started to straighten up and then remembered what had happened in New York, so I made a thorough search of my own. But he hadn't planted anything in the room, so he'd probably hoped to find some evidence of what I had accomplished or hoped to accomplish.

When I finally had the room straightened up, I put a chair against the door to make sure Eddie didn't slip back in. Then I stretched out on the bed and went to sleep.

Two hours later I awakened, feeling a little better. I took a shower and shaved and felt much better. I was to pick up Lisette for a late lunch, but I still had a little time. I called Lieutenant Stern again.

"Busy?" I asked when he came on.

"No," he said. "I'm just sitting here waiting for you to solve the rest of the case for me."

"Sorry," I said. "You should have told me. I just took a nap, but I would have forced myself if I had known."

"Pretty soft life," he said. "Maybe I'll resign and get a job as an insurance dick. You got anything more?

"Not a thing," I said cheerfully. "I had another talk with Lane, hoping there might have been something connecting the two guys to the likes of Eddie Capo. But if there is, he doesn't know anything about it."

"I already tried that," the Lieutenant said. "I went over everything they did from the time they arrived here. Not once but twice. It always ended up sounding like any three tourists."

"You got anything else?" I asked.

"No. I told you I'm checking on boats, but no results yet. I've got a man keeping an eye on Perrin and another tailing Eddie Capo. By the way, he called in not long ago and said that Eddie visited your hotel and that he had a swollen mouth when he left."

"We had a small argument," I said.

"I can see that one of you will be providing more work for me before this is over," he said.

"Something I did want to ask you," I said. "Why do you suppose the killer went to all that trouble getting the two bodies buried? Why didn't he just push them into one of the quicksand pits?"

"While it's true that we might never find a body in one of those pits, there is also no guarantee we wouldn't find it the first time we started probing. There's no way the killer could depend on it."

"Okay," I said. "Keep digging."

"What do you think I do all day?" he demanded. "And I have a few other cases here, too."

I said good-bye and hung up. Then I went down to Bourbon Street to meet Lisette. She was just arriving at the restaurant as I got there.

"There's nothing I like so much as a prompt woman," I told her, "unless it's a prompt woman who also happens to be beautiful."

"I was hungry," she said.

"Women are too realistic," I announced. "You might at least have let me think you were prompt because you couldn't wait any longer to see me. You have no romance in your soul."

We went inside and were led to a table. The waiter went away to bring us a couple of martinis.

"I just read in the paper," she said, "about those two men who were killed on some little island and then secretly buried here in the city. Is that the case you're working on, Milo?"

"That's it, honey. And I wish that somebody else had it."

"Aren't you making any progress?"

"Not that you can notice," I said. "I have a theory that it's tied in with the drug traffic in some way, but that's as far as I've gotten."

"Drugs?" she said, making a face. "I thought the drug traffic was just something that the tabloids thought up when there was a dull day in the news."

"It's real enough. Remember the guy that was following you the night you came to my apartment?" She nodded. "Well, the cops caught up with him. He was a drug peddler. Also a rapist, so it's just as well you came tapping at my door. In fact, I'm so grateful to him, I thought of passing the hat for his defense."

She laughed. "Was he really all that? I thought he was just another of those sick characters one meets every so often."

The waiter came with the martinis and I waited until he was gone. "He was sick, all right," I said. "But then who isn't? It used to be a couch was the place for a seduction; now it's a place to talk about your seduction."

"But those men were here looking for pirate treasure," she said. "Maybe they found it and that's why they were killed."

"I doubt it. There are probably a lot of pirates around, but they keep their treasure in the bank."

"Oh, people are always finding old coins and things all over Louisiana," she said.

"Sure they are," I said. "But I think I'm the only person who has really found a treasure."

"Why, thank you, sir," she said.

"I'm sorry I can't see you tonight," I told her. "I have to work. But I won't make a habit of it."

"It's just as well, Milo," she said. "I couldn't see you tonight anyway."

"Why?" I demanded. "Another guy?"

"No. I have to go somewhere. And I won't be back until day after tomorrow."

"Hey, you can't do that to me. That will mean about forty-eight hours that I won't see you. And when I've just discovered you, too."

"You'll live through it," she said, reaching over and patting me on the hand. "And I'll see you day after tomorrow. That is, if you don't find another girl by then."

"Please," I said. "I'm the faithful dog type. I'll be here pining away, drowning my sorrow in drink—which reminds me that we need two more drinks." I signaled the waiter to bring us two more. "Where are you going?"

"Upstate," she said. "I promised to do a favor for a friend of mine who has offices up there. I made the promise some time ago and I have to keep it."

"I'll phone you every hour," I said.

"No," she said, laughing. "I won't tell you where I'll be, so you can't. I'll be back before you've even missed me, silly."

We finished our second drink and had lunch. I took her

back to her apartment. She promised that she'd call me the minute she returned. Then I went back to the Royal House. I stopped near the hotel and bought some clothes that would be suitable for tramping over a swampy island.

I spent the rest of the afternoon in the hotel bar. Peter Lane was still there, getting stoned and alternately bemoaning the fate of his friends and the fact that the police still wouldn't let him leave New Orleans. Later I had dinner in the dining room and then I went upstairs and changed clothes. I was down at the docks a few minutes before nine.

Narcisse Coillon and Willie Morell arrived a few minutes after I did. Willie was loaded down with various things, including a forked stick, a number of stakes, and a clothes-line. Coillon had brought two powerful electric lanterns. We found West Carroll waiting on his boat. We got aboard and he cast off.

"I see," he said finally, "they found those two guys."

"Yeah," I said, "so I guess they didn't just fall into the quicksand."

"But who would have thought such a thing would happen?" Coillon said. "They were strangers here and knew no one."

"Well, someone knew them well enough to kill them," I pointed out. "You and Carroll both know the island and the locality. Don't either of you have an idea of how it could have been done?"

"The only way," the boatman said, "would be what you yourself suggested. A rowboat. I would have heard a motor-boat. So would the others. There was no other motor near there the night we were. I could swear to that."

"I, too," said the guide. "But why was such a thing done? Perhaps they had something to do with some married women in the city. There are men in New Orleans who would kill because of that."

"There are men everywhere who will," I said. "But I doubt if that was it. Even if it was, why pick this spot? And if it was someone who found out they were coming to the island that night, how could he know that the two men would wander off alone? Another thing: you were more than an hour late in getting here. Would the killer have waited that long? Wouldn't he have decided that the plans had been changed and have given up?"

"It is for the police to answer such weighty questions," Coillon said. "I have enough to do to make a living without worrying about such things."

"Me, too," West Carroll grunted. "They'll worry about it. They were out this afternoon checking all the rowboats and small outboard motorboats."

"What do you think about it, Willie?" I asked.

"Many bad spirits on that island, sir," he said. I saw the flash of white teeth in the running lights of the boat.

"Willie's got the answer," Carroll said.

"They're not just on the island," I said. "If I get an afternoon off one day, Carroll, will you take me skin diving?"

"If you want to hire me," he said.

"You furnish the equipment?" I asked.

"Yeah. Everything but the swimming trunks. You'll have to bring your own. You ever done it?"

"A couple of times," I said.

A few minutes later, he swung the boat into shore and we were at the island. It was pretty dark, but even so I could see that the island was bleak. I couldn't see to tell how large it was, but it didn't seem to be much. In the center of it was a hill which was silhouetted against the sky. There were a couple of scrubby trees on it.

Coillon and Willie jumped over the prow of the boat as soon as she stopped, and Coillon held the light while I jumped.

"Don't forget to get back here in time," West Carroll said.

"We'll be back," I told him. "If you think we're going to be late, just yell and we'll come whether we're through or not."

"You want to just start looking for buried treasure?" Coillon asked me.

"No, let's go first to about the spot you were when the two men decided to go their own way."

He turned and tramped off to the right with Willie and me following. I had one of the electric lanterns and I swung it around so I could see what the island was like. It was pretty poor-looking. There were tufts of dwarfed grass, an occasional small tree, and scattered shrubs. From what I was seeing, the Lieutenant was right when he said it was no place to hide anything.

We went about a hundred yards before Coillon came to a stop. "We were about here and Willie was using his divining stick when they decided to go the other way," he said.

"Where'd they go?" I asked.

"That way," he said, pointing back the way we came, "only they cut in close to the hill instead of following the shoreline."

"They had a light?"

"One just like you're carrying."

"Okay," I said. "Let's go on to the spot you were at when you heard one of them yell."

We walked on about another two hundred yards, maybe a little more. "Guess it was about here," he said. "It took us longer that night because Willie was divining. We were about here, and Willie was out in front with his stick. Right, Willie?"

"Yes, sir. I was goin' along with my divining rod just like this—" He lifted the forked stick until it was parallel to the ground and walked slowly forward. Suddenly he seemed to trip and almost fall. "Well, I'll be jinks swing," he said. "For a minute, I thinks we find that treasure. But I guess it was just one of them spirits grabbing at the rod. They does that sometimes."

"Maybe you just tripped," I suggested.

"No, sir. That was a spirit. I knows."

"Okay. Which direction did the yell come from?"

"On the other side of the hill," Coillon said, pointing.

"Let's go around to where they were when the yell came. As near as you can make it."

"Might as well go straight ahead," he said. "It'll be just as close as going back." He set off.

"You wants me to do a little divining as we goes along?" Willie asked as we followed.

"Not especially," I said. "Will that thing really locate anything, Willie?"

"Yes, sir."

"Did you ever find any treasure?"

"Millions of dollars. Old coins, big sparklers, all kinds of stuff. But gotta watch out for them spirits. Why, I knows a man he goes to dig up a treasure, only he ain't careful like I am, and when he digs the hole the first thing he knows, out comes a big ol' rooster crowing his fool head off and vanishes in a big puff of smoke. Then a whole passel of chickens come out one by one and they vanishes just like the rooster. And the last thing to come out of that hole was a big bull with smoke and fire coming out of his mouth and ears. And that man what was looking for the treasure, he went as crazy as a bessie bug. Yes, sir."

"Is that the truth, Willie?" I asked, grinning.

"Yes, sir. I don't tell nothin' but the truth, because God don't like ugly."

"That's a good reason," I admitted. "Are you married, Willie?"

"No, sir. Married got teeth."

"I know a lot of people who would agree with you," I said, "although I doubt if they could put it so succinctly."

"Maybe they just pushes too many words on top of what they is thinking," he said. "Sometimes a man got more words than he knows what to do with and then they starts pushin' fire."

"I think you got it right, Willie," I said. "How much farther, Coillon?"

"Not much," he grunted.

While I'd been talking to Willie, I'd kept looking around, and the rest of the island seemed to have the same appearance as the section where we landed. It certainly would be a good place to hide treasure; it wasn't good for anything else.

"Where are all the quicksand pits?" I asked Coillon.

"We've passed six or seven," he said dryly. "And there are even more around on the other side. I'll show them to you."

We walked another three or four hundred yards and Coillon stopped. "I'd guess the yell came from somewhere near here," he said. "And right over there are two quicksand pits." He flashed the light to his left.

I could see what looked like two big mudholes separated by several feet of dry ground with tufts of grass on it. I walked over to the edge of one of them. Even near and with the light on it, it still looked like just another big mudhole. I said as much.

"That's what fools a lot of people," Coillon said. "They step into it and then it's too late."

"So quickly?" I asked.

"If you don't have anything solid to grab and pull yourself out," he said. "You can't just walk out. Stuff sucks you right down."

I flashed the light down near my feet and something caught my eye. I bent down and looked at the ground. There was a dark brown stain on the ground at my feet. I couldn't be sure, but it looked very much like blood. I set my lantern against the trunk of a scrawny tree and squatted down, taking out my handkerchief. I scooped up the dirt with the stain and wrapped it in my handkerchief.

"What are you doing?" Coillon asked.

I reached for my lantern and noticed something move on

the trunk of the tree. At first I thought it was hair, but looking closer I saw it was only a few strands of twine. I picked up the lantern and walked back.

"What did you say?" I asked Coillon.

"I wondered what you were doing? Did you find something?"

"No," I said. "Nothing to do with the case. I just saw an unusual-looking rock and I got it to take back with me. Sort of a hobby of mine."

He grunted.

"Let's go look at the shoreline," I said. "Is it this way?"

He turned and walked in the way I had indicated. I fell into step with him. It was no more than thirty yards or so to the edge of the water. I walked along it for several yards, flashing the light at my feet. Then I reversed myself and went the other way for several yards.

"No sign of any boat being drawn up here," I said.

"Of course not," Coillon said. There was an edge of contempt in his voice. "If anyone did land here in a rowboat, they wouldn't bring it up out of the water. And even if they were stupid enough to do that, the marks would have been washed out in the past two weeks."

"I suppose so," I admitted. But I continued to walk along looking at the ground near the edge of the water. Coillon and Willie followed behind me. Coillon didn't say any more. I was paying him, so he was going to humor me.

Then I saw something. It was only a small mark in the ground at the very edge of the water, but when I squatted down to look at it, there was no doubt that it was part of a heel mark, as though made by a man walking out of the water. Coillon had stopped beside me and I pointed to it. He bent down to look.

"Somebody's been here," he said. "But I can tell you that wasn't made two weeks ago. Probably somebody else looking for treasure."

He was probably right. Anyway, I knew that there wasn't enough of it for the police to make a cast and find anybody. I straightened up.

"Are there really many people who seriously look for pirate treasure?" I asked him.

"Thousands of them," he said. "That's what I mostly guide, people looking for treasure. And I'm not the only guide in New Orleans, just as Willie's not the only diviner. There are even a couple of men who use radio and electronic devices that they claim will locate treasure. Sure, they take it seriously. Maybe seriously enough to kill."

"Is that going to be your new theory?" I asked. "That they were killed for the treasure they never found?"

"They had a map, didn't they?" he asked. "I saw it myself. Maybe somebody wanted the map."

"Why?"

"To find the treasure. Nobody's looked on this island for a long time. I remember hearing that it was once thought there was treasure here, but I don't remember anybody wanting to look here since I've been guiding. Until those three men came along with their map. Maybe they flashed the map around New Orleans and maybe somebody followed us out here. Maybe they even got it. You know where that map is right now?"

I didn't. I hadn't even thought about the confounded map. Personally, I thought the whole treasure-hunting idea was crazy, but I had to admit that people went in for even crazier things and sometimes killed over them.

"Maybe you've got something," I said. "And maybe not. We'll see."

"Don't you want me to do no divining?" Willie asked. "If they is any treasure here, I finds it. But we gotta talk to all them spirits. They's lots of them here. I can feel them hanging around just as nervy as a gnat."

"Well … ," I said.

There was a shout from the end of the island. "Hey, you want to go back with me, you'd better be coming."

"Coming," I shouted back. "Sorry, Willie, I guess we'll have to talk to the spirits another time. Let's go."

The three of us followed the shoreline around until we came to the boat in about another fifteen minutes. Carroll stood at the prow of the boat and helped us aboard.

"Well, did you find any treasure?" he asked as he started the motor and cast off.

"Mr. March found a heel print," Coillon said with no expression in his voice. "And a rock he liked."

Carroll looked at me and I could see the grin on his face. "Well, that's more than most treasure hunters find."

"And less than two hunters found a little more than two weeks ago," I added. "You know damn well I didn't come out here to look for treasure. And I didn't find much of anything else—except Coillon's theory that they were killed for their treasure map."

"Maybe," Carroll said. "Some of these nuts that come down here would do anything if they thought they'd find golden doubloons. Tourists!"

"You make your living from them, don't you?" I asked.

"Yeah, but that don't mean I have to like them."

"Are you a Native Son?" I asked.

"No. Coillon, there, his family's been here for three hundred years. I'm practically a tourist myself, but I like it here."

"You must do pretty well," I said. "Boats like this aren't available in any of the cut-rate stores I know."

"I do all right," he said. "The tourists pay well to be taken on fool errands and to learn skin diving."

We were all silent the rest of the way back to the dock. When the boat nosed up against the pier, I got out my money and paid Carroll. Then I followed Coillon and Willie off the boat.

"I'll be seeing you in a day or two to go skin diving," I called back to Carroll.

"Okay," he said. He was already backing the boat away from the pier.

"You want us anymore?" Coillon asked.

"Not tonight," I said. "If I decide to take another trip, I'll get in touch with you. Willie, if you have a little time, I'd like to learn more about how you fight off the spirits. I'll pay you for your time."

"Yes, sir," he said.

"Well … good night," Coillon said. "Willie, you'll be around in the next day or two?"

"Yes, sir, I sure will, Mr. Coillon."

"Good night," I said. I watched Coillon walk down the pier and disappear in the shadows. A moment later he reappeared beyond them in the street light. I turned and looked out on the Mississippi. The red and green lights of Carroll's boat were plainly visible. He was heading in what I was pretty sure was the direction of the Gulf. I wondered where he was picking up his customers that he had to meet so urgently.

I started to walk along the pier and Willie fell into step with me.

"Willie " I asked, "do you only work for Coillon?"

"No, sir. I works for any guide that wants to use me. Sometimes it's Mr. Coillon, sometimes it's somebody else. I only works maybe three, four months a year."

"Do you work for Coillon a lot?"

"Sometimes do, sometimes don't."

I stopped and lit a cigarette. "Willie," I said, "you're a big phony."

"What you means?" he asked.

"You know damn well what I mean," I said. "You're putting on a big act with this business of playing the poor, dumb black boy, ignorant and superstitious. I suppose it's good for the tourist trade and maybe even makes it better for you with Coillon, but it doesn't go over with me."

"You is pilin' up them words," he said.

"Drop it, Willie," I said. "I knew you were acting up a storm yesterday when you picked me up on the martini bit. And tonight when you knew what I meant when I used a word like *succinctly*. I may be an ofay, but I know that no cotton-picking burr-head is going to know that martinis on Madison

Avenue means lemon peel or is going to know the meaning of *succinctly*. You dig me, chum?"

He looked at me for a minute, then started chuckling. "I knew I'd made a mistake with you both times," he said, and his voice had taken on a new clarity, "but it was too late. Oh, well, you win a few and lose a few."

"All right," I said, "what's the gag?"

"I'm going to school up North," he said. "University of Michigan. I come down here and work as a diviner because I can make more money at it than anything else I would do, and it's putting me through school. And the tourists, not to mention the local quality folk, like to have their black boys be burr-heads. It makes them feel good. Then when he's something like a diviner, they can run home and talk about the colorful character they met. Sometimes they're even so impressed they tip me in addition to my pay. You won't give me away, will you, Mr. March?"

"I'm a professional snooper, not a professional squealer," I said. "And the name is Milo."

"Well, you have to admit I do the diviner bit pretty good," he said.

"Good enough to be booked on Ed Sullivan," I said. "All right, now that we're down to cases, I want to know something. That business of telling those three marks from New York that the only time to go to the island was at night. Was that window dressing or did somebody tell you to say it?"

"Coillon wanted me to tell them that."

"Why?"

"He said he had another job for the afternoon and didn't

want to give it up. I didn't mind. The act looks even better at night anyway. I was beginning to get my feelings hurt because you wouldn't let me put it on tonight."

"I know," I said, laughing. "Is there anything that you know about this case that I don't? I know you might not have been able to say anything in front of Coillon."

"No," he said. "It happened just as they've been telling you."

"Okay," I said. "You were raised in New Orleans?"

"Yes."

"Know it well?"

"Sure."

"Can you drive a car?"

"Yes."

"How would you like to work for me the rest of the time I'm here?"

"I'd like it fine, but I'll have to stay in character when we're around other people."

"I'll understand," I said. "But watch some of those lines or you'll break me up. Okay, you'll start tomorrow. Call me at the Royal House about eleven o'clock and I'll tell you when to start. That'll give you time to tell Coillon you're working."

"Okay."

"All right, let's go. We'll grab a cab and I'll drop you off at your home."

"No," he said. "Better not. There's still a lot of people around here who don't know the meaning of the word *integration*. I'll leave you here. It'll be better that way. And I'll call you tomorrow. ... And thanks."

"Okay," I said.

He turned and started down the street that ran along the side of the river. "I will be mighty proud to work for you, sir," he called back. "Yes, sir. I likes to keep busy. Too much sit down breaks a man's pants." Then he was gone.

I went straight up the street, figuring I'd find a cab in a couple of blocks. I'd gone about half a block when a car came sweeping up the street behind me. It swung into the curb and braked smoothly to a stop beside me. The front door swung open.

"Get in, sucker," a voice said.

It was Eddie Capo. He was holding a gun, firmly pointed at me.

EIGHT

The motor of the black Cadillac purred softly and peacefully in the background while Eddie Capo, his mouth still swollen, stared at me over the top of his gun. I stared back at him, wondering whether to try my luck then or later. Under my breath, I was cursing myself for having been careless enough to let him slip up on me. I hadn't been expecting him to move so quickly, but that was no excuse.

"You want to argue about it, sucker?" he asked. "I'd like nothing better. But the boss says to bring you to see him, and no shooting. Only if you want to argue, the boss can't say I'm wrong."

I looked at him, weighing his words. He was probably telling the truth. Otherwise he would have started shooting before I even looked around. Men like Eddie Capo never make the mistake of giving anyone an even break.

"You getting in, sucker," Eddie asked, "or you want to try to be a big man?"

"I'm getting in," I said. "Why not? I know you wouldn't shoot me unless my back was turned." I climbed into the seat beside him and closed the door.

"Keep it up, chum," he said. "You don't worry me. Sooner or later, the boss is going to say go ahead and it's going to be a pleasure to take you. Now, just hold it." He reached over with his left hand and patted my coat. Then he reached in and snaked my gun out of its holster. He put it in his pocket on the far side from me.

"Maybe you'll get it back," he said. "Just sit nice and quiet and you won't get hurt." He slipped his own gun back into its holster and started the car.

We drove through the winding streets, cutting around corners, so that I had no idea where we were going. Finally he cut into a driveway leading to a huge white house with giant pillars in front of it. Sitting well back from the street, surrounded by huge trees, it looked like something out of the feudal past. Eddie drove the car around in back of the house and stopped.

"You the joker who told the cops to put a tail on me?" he asked as he turned off the motor.

"No," I said. "I knew they had put one on you, though."

"I shook him," he said contemptuously. "Cops. They never saw the day they could tail Eddie Capo."

"I am the joker, however," I said, "who told the cops not to pull you in for questioning. I told them I wanted to handle you myself. You're beginning to get in my hair, Eddie. Every time I turn around, I see you. I'm getting tired of it."

"It's going to be a pleasure," he repeated. "I owe you something for this afternoon. Get out, chum."

I opened the door and got out. Eddie slid out after me, his hand close to his gun. He motioned me in through the back door. I went. We were in a long hall leading up to what was obviously the front door. On the left, near the front, there was a winding staircase.

"Go straight ahead," Eddie said. "Then we're going up the stairs to the next floor. And take it easy."

I walked down the hallway and then went up the stairs. When I reached the top, I stopped.

"The second door on the right," Eddie said. "Just open it and go in. But remember I'll be right behind you."

I obeyed, wondering if this was going to be more hanky-panky with no lights. I opened the door and stepped into a study that might have come out of the Napoleonic era. Everything in it was antique, looking as if it were in as good a condition as the day it had been bought. Even the books that covered one wall were all specially bound and looked as old as the furniture.

"Here he is, boss," Eddie said from behind me.

Then I saw the man. He was sitting in a huge chair behind an Empire-period desk. I'd been right about one thing; he was old. Probably seventy but well preserved, and his cheeks still had a ruddy glow. His head was completely bald. Heavy-rimmed glasses sat firmly on his nose. His was a strong face, strong enough so that even age had not weakened it. He held a cigar in a carefully manicured hand, and there was a glass of brandy in front of him.

"Good evening, Mr. March," he said. It was the same voice I'd heard in my room that night. "Thank you for coming to see me."

"Did I have a choice?" I asked.

Eddie laughed behind me. "I pulled his teeth, boss. He was carrying a .32 in a shoulder holster. Just like a big boy."

"Thank you, Eddie," the old man said. "Won't you sit down, Mr. March?" He indicated a chair near his desk.

I went over and sat down. It was his party; I was going to let him announce the games.

"Would you like a brandy, Mr. March?" he asked. "I can recommend this particular brandy. It's a very old import."

"I like brandy," I said.

"Serve Mr. March, Eddie," the old man said.

Eddie didn't like the idea, but he went to a cabinet against the wall and got out a brandy snifter and poured a generous splash into it from a bottle that looked old and musty. He brought it over to me.

"You may leave us now, Eddie," the old man said. "I will ring for you when we have concluded."

"Don't you think I ought to stay, boss?" Eddie asked. "This guy likes to think he's tough."

"You may leave us, Eddie," the old man said firmly.

"Okay," Eddie said. He glanced at me and went out. The old man continued to wait until I had tasted my brandy. I could see he was waiting for some reaction.

"It's an excellent brandy," I said.

He practically beamed. "I was sure you would enjoy it," he said. "It takes a palate to appreciate a fine brandy, but somehow I was sure you had one. Now, I'm aware that I have a slight advantage over you, so let me correct it by introducing myself. I am Raoul Rouen. The last of a very old family in New Orleans. Creole, of course."

"Of course," I said. *"Sorti de la cuisse de Jupiter."*

"Exactly," he said, beaming. "I was sure that you would understand such things. It's really a pity that we have to be enemies."

"Are we?" I asked.

"Someday," he said, "I would like to have the pleasure of showing you over this house. It was built by my great-grandfather. Every bit of furniture was brought over here from Europe. My mother was born in the front bedroom on the next floor. I was also born there. They do not build houses like this anymore, Mr. March. Nor appreciate them. This room, for example. Some of my most pleasant hours have been spent here."

"It is a very attractive room," I said, looking around. It was, too.

"Do you like that?" he asked, gesturing toward one wall. I looked. There was a painting on the wall. Of a field. Just a field, but it had color and movement and warmth. And a kind of strength, too. I said as much, and the old man beamed again.

"I painted it," he said. "In southern France fifty-two years ago. I was considered quite promising. I won a number of scholarships, as a matter of fact."

"A pity you didn't stay with it," I said.

He gestured with the cigar. "Do you have any idea how much a painter makes? I couldn't even support myself on it, to say nothing of this house."

"Picasso does all right," I commented.

"Ah, yes, but Picasso is a showman as well as a painter. I was only a painter. Do you know how many painters—great painters—have starved all their lives?"

"Many," I admitted.

"Of course. This was not for me. So when the family fortune

was suddenly gone when I was only twenty-five, I had to find other means to secure the money I needed. Among other things, it was my duty to keep this house as it has always been. I have done that, Mr. March."

"I can see that," I said. "And you have no children?"

"None."

"And what will happen to this when you are gone?" He looked around the room fiercely, then smiled at me wryly. "I suppose it can be turned into quite a number of excellent hot dog stands."

"It hardly seems worthwhile, does it?" I asked.

He was silent for a minute, staring at the desk, lost in some inner thought. Finally he looked up at me and his face had hardened somewhat. "Tonight, Mr. March, is by way of being a milestone in my life," he said. "In a way, you are honored, although you may not appreciate it, by being invited to my home to meet me face to face. Do you believe in fate, Mr. March?"

"I do, as long as I can control it," I said.

He smiled. "I said much the same when I was your age. Now I'm not so sure. Many things have changed, and I find I don't care too much. I am about at the end of my life. Perhaps that makes it easier to accept things as they come. Even fate. I have had a feeling since meeting you the other evening that fate is about to take a hand in my last few pages. That is why you were asked to come here. ... Tell me, Mr. March, as a favor to an old man, what you think you know about me."

"When I first encountered Eddie Capo," I said, "I asked a friend in the New York Police Department who Eddie was working for now. He told me that Eddie was supposed to work for a man who was one of the top members of the Syndicate, a man who was known to only a handful of the top men of the underworld and to the rest was known as 'The Painter.' There is no doubt in my mind that you are that man. I think that you represent the Syndicate in this area in all their operations. And I think that the two men in whom I am interested somehow accidentally bumped into some part of those operations and were killed as a result of it."

"You left out the traffic in drugs," he said.

"I said *all* their operations," I answered. "I'm sure that drugs are your chief business in this area."

"A neat summation of my business interest," he said. He sipped his brandy. "I started in this business, Mr. March, fifty years ago. In a small way, of course. In those days there was no such thing as what you call the Syndicate. I worked for a man, and in due course of time inherited his interest and this was my territory. Those were the days when there was considerable violence, which threatened the profits. Several of us saw the wisdom of pooling our interest to the point of mutual self-protection. That was the beginning of the Syndicate— although it might be more accurate to call it Limited Partners. I look after my partners' interest in my territory and they look after mine in theirs. It has been a most profitable arrangement. I have made a lot of money on it and have paid taxes on every cent of it. I pride myself on being a good citizen."

"I doubt," I said dryly, "that making drug addicts out of thousands of people is one of the attributes of good citizenship."

"Not my responsibility," he said, waving his hand as though to push it away. "Do you claim that the owner of an oil refinery is responsible for all the fools who kill themselves and others by driving recklessly? Of course not. I have merely served a taste which already existed long before I was born."

"Okay," I said, knowing there was no point in arguing with him.

"Ask anyone in New Orleans," he said, "and they will express only horror at the idea that Raoul Rouen might have anything to do with the world we're talking about. I have kept my two lives successfully apart for fifty years. But that time is over. I have recently had two visits from members of the Federal Bureau of Investigation. They have no proof, but they know. It is only a matter of time until my identity will be better known. I have a feeling that you may be instrumental in speeding that time up. But none of that is too important to me. My remaining years are few in number. The things which I have held dear and struggled to maintain are mostly worthless to the rest of the world and will be gone not long after I am."

"The world changes," I said, "but not always for the worse, although it may seem so to those caught in the change. I assume, however, that all of this conversation has some relationship to me?"

"Yes," he said. He smiled. "Sometimes I forget that we must get down to business quickly. You know, you shouldn't have treated Eddie the way you did this afternoon."

"Then he should stay out of my room."

"I sent him there, in the hopes that there might be some indication of what progress you have made. I was aware that you were responsible for locating the bodies of the two men, and I thought you might have uncovered other things."

"Such as?"

He smiled again. "Things which do not concern your work. Eddie reported that he found nothing."

"Of course not. Anything I learn will be kept in my head or turned over to others. And keep Eddie Capo away from me or he'll get worse than I gave him this afternoon."

"That was still unwise," he said. "Eddie is now most eager to kill you. He says that sooner or later I will permit it. I suppose he's right. But I dislike killings. I prefer other methods whenever possible."

"And the two men who were killed?" I asked gently.

He flushed. "I told you that I did not order that, and that it was done without my knowledge. Had I been told about the situation, I would have handled it differently."

"What was the situation?"

He smiled and shrugged to indicate that he had no intention of telling me.

"I know that they had to stumble onto something that concerns you, although they were probably unaware of what they knew. Was it somewhere in the city or on the island?"

"Your assumption is quite correct," he said. "Your question is one which I shall not answer. Mr. March, I prefer not to fight you. Is there not some way that I can prevail on you to leave well enough alone? Your Mr. Lane had nothing to do with the deaths of his two friends. Your company is interested only in that. Your duty could be satisfied and at the same time I could make it well worth your time."

"You don't have that much money," I said. "But there is a way you can get rid of me."

"How?"

"Turn over to me or the police the man or men who murdered those two men, with sufficient evidence. Do that and I'll leave the rest of your activities to your conscience and the FBI."

"You know that is quite impossible," he said reprovingly. "It's not a question of loyalty, but of good business. I have many persons working for me. Should I treat one in such a manner, none of the others would trust me."

"Then we're right back where we started," I said. I finished my brandy. "And I'm wasting your time."

He made a gesture. "Wait, Mr. March. Perhaps we can reach another agreement. I am told that you are a man who keeps his word, a rarity in this age. Suppose you give me your word that if you come across evidence of other activities of mine, you will come to me before you go to the police. If you do that, I will keep hands off so far as your work on the murder is concerned. That does not mean I will control all of those who work for me, but I will give no orders to stop you."

"No dice," I said, shaking my head. "I can't promise you anything of the sort. You claim that all of this happened because of a weakness in your organization; somebody acted without orders. But two men died. Let's not forget that. We know about these two. How many others have died that your business might profit, Mr. Rouen? How many dead that we don't know about? How much blood is smeared over these fine antiques of yours, how much blood is in this rare brandy we're drinking?"

"Mr. March, you disappoint me," he said. "You are talking like a moralist rather than an intelligent man."

"Of course I'm a moralist," I said roughly. "No one has to be stupid to have moral values any more than they have to be intelligent to be amoral. If I weren't a moralist, Eddie Capo would have been killed this afternoon instead of knocked down. Of course I'll kill when my own life is at stake, but I will not kill for either pleasure or profit."

"Very well," he said. One hand went beneath his desk and I was sure he was ringing for Eddie. "I am sorry, Mr. March. I had hoped that you and I might reach some sort of agreement. I am sure that I would enjoy knowing you better. One of the unfortunate aspects of my business is the paucity of people to talk with. And most of the people in New Orleans are my inferiors. It has made for a lonely life."

I lit a cigarette and stared at him through the smoke. "Mr. Rouen, I am sorry for you. The world you cling to never really existed except in your mind. To keep that fantasy, you have poured all kinds of filth into the real world."

His mouth tightened and he stared straight ahead at the door. A moment later it opened and Eddie Capo came in.

"Mr. March," the old man said, "is ready to leave. We have concluded our discussion."

"Mr. March," I said, "would also like to have his gun back. I don't want it being used by someone and then the blame put on me."

"Give him his gun, Eddie."

"Okay," Eddie said. He took the gun from his pocket and tossed it to me. I caught it and slipped it back into my holster without looking at it. "I took the shells out of it, snooper."

"I was sure you would," I told him. I got up and walked over to the door.

"What do I do with him, boss?" Eddie asked.

"Return him to his hotel," the old man said. "Safely." He was still looking at me.

"Okay," Eddie said. But he sounded disappointed. "Can I just rough him up a little? To teach him something."

"No."

Eddie shrugged and looked at me. "You're still riding that luck, sucker. But it won't last."

"Maybe," I said. I started out of the room.

"Mr. March," the old man said.

I stopped and turned to look at him. He was staring at a point just above my right shoulder.

"I am well aware," he said, "that you have been working closely with the police, which in many respects makes it dangerous to make a move against you. I am also aware that you cannot solve the deaths of the two men without hurting me and my organization. From now on, Mr. March, you will be watched every minute of the day and the night by some member of my organization. You will get no more warnings. The minute that you even seem about to stumble onto anything about my affairs—you will be killed."

NINE

He continued to stare over my shoulder as he finished speaking, and I knew that he was trying to recapture his vision and erase the pictures I had put in his mind. He'd succeed, too. He'd had fifty years of practice. Maybe even generations, for his ancestors must have been not too different, and this beautiful house had probably been built on the backs of slaves. There was no point in saying any more to him, and I didn't even try.

"Take him home, Eddie," the old man said. He sounded tired.

"Get going, sucker," Eddie said, prodding me in the shoulder.

I turned and went out, walking down the stairs, then back through the long corridor and out to the car. I got in the front seat and Eddie went around to the other side and slid under the steering wheel.

We drove back to the hotel with neither of us talking. Eddie stopped the big Cadillac in front of the entrance.

"I'll be seeing you," he said. Eddie was going to wait like the well-trained dog that he was, but he wasn't going to let me forget that he had me marked for his own.

"Yeah," I said. I didn't feel like trading badinage with Eddie at the moment. The visit to the big white house and listening to the old man talk had depressed me. I got out of the car and went into the hotel without looking back.

It was late, but the bar was still open, with a dozen or so customers still at it. I went in and found a spot that wasn't too close to the others and ordered a double shot of Canadian Club. When it came I downed it fast and ordered another. I drank the second one more slowly. There was a blonde with the crowd who wanted to play games, but I wasn't interested. I had one more drink and then I went upstairs and to sleep.

I was up early the next morning and had breakfast downstairs in the coffee shop. Then I took a cab downtown and went in to see Lieutenant Stern. I told him about the trip to the island the night before and gave him the dirt I'd wrapped up in my handkerchief.

"Just see if that's human blood, if you will," I said. "It won't buy us anything except that we'll know where they were killed and it might come in handy later."

"You can find the spot again?" he asked.

"I think so," I said. "I don't think there was anything else to find. The ground was too hard there to show any footprints."

"Okay," he said. "I'll send it into the lab. We drew a blank on the boat checkup, but I didn't expect much. And my man lost Eddie Capo."

"I know," I said. "You know an old guy named Raoul Rouen?"

"I know of him," he said, "but I can hardly say that I know him. The Rouens were one of the first families in New Orleans. It is doubtful if they would have talked to the Cabots and Lodges, if you know what I mean. He's the last of the bunch and just seems to live in the old house with his memories. Why? He have something to do with this?"

"Everything," I said, "but I can't prove it at the moment."

"It'll take a lot of proof in this town," he said. "But I've gotten to the point where nothing surprises me. Want to talk about it?"

"Not yet," I told him, "but I will soon. I'll check with you during the day."

I left and went looking for a car rental office. I was getting tired of taking cabs all the time, and it wouldn't cost Intercontinental any more to rent a car. I found one and gave a deposit on a Cadillac and drove it away. I stopped at a drugstore long enough to look at the phone directory. Then I drove on downtown a few blocks and parked.

There was a big, sandy-haired man in the office I visited. He was young enough to look as if he hadn't been out of college long. But he had to have a lot on the ball if he was sitting in that office.

"What can I do for you?" he asked politely as I came in.

"I'd like to get some information," I said.

His face hardened. "What sort of information?" he asked.

I grinned at him. "Relax," I said. I reached into my pocket and brought out my wallet. "First, I'm Milo March. I'm an insurance investigator, currently working for Intercontinental Insurance. Here are my credentials. I'm also a Major in the Army Reserves and was formerly attached to Central Intelligence Agency. Here's my card on that with both picture and fingerprints if you'd like to check them. And here's a card that shows my security classification."

He examined all the cards and then looked at me. "These are all very nice," he said, "but they don't really buy you anything with this bureau. What is it you want, Mr. March?"

"I didn't say they bought me anything," I said. "I showed them for identification. Now, to what I want. I know that at least two Federal agencies have been interested in certain criminal activities here in New Orleans, especially the drug trade. I am down here working on the murder of two men on Placide Island a little more than two weeks ago. The bodies were just discovered day before yesterday. I believe that my case may be somewhat related to the case you people are hoping to make."

"So?" he asked.

"Forget what the Attorney General told you about strangers asking questions," I said with a grin. "If you're worried about me, call General Norton at the CIA in Washington and ask him about me. His language will probably cause the operator to cut you off, but I'm sure you'll be able to translate."

He finally grinned. "That isn't necessary, Mr. March," he said. "I know your name and I know a little bit about you. But even that doesn't make much difference. We still can't turn our files over to you for the benefit of private business."

"I wasn't asking you to. But maybe you can help me just a little and then maybe I can help you quite a bit more."

"Tell me what you know and I'll see what I can do."

"Only don't find it necessary to ask permission in triplicate first," I said. "Now, I know you've been working on this down here and I suspect you haven't made much progress. I know that you've had your eye on a man named Raoul Rouen here, who you're pretty certain is the local Syndicate man and in charge of all the drug smuggling through the port of New Orleans."

"Who told you that?" he asked me sharply.

"Rouen," I said, grinning at him. "I wasn't even asking you to verify that. But I would like to know why you haven't pulled him in."

He thought about it a minute and decided he could answer. "We have no proof," he said. "We do have testimony that Rouen is an important member of what is known as the Syndicate, but we have no proof of that. And we have not yet been able to get any proof connecting him with the smuggling or subsequent handling of narcotics."

"He just sits up at that old house?" I guessed.

He nodded. "In the past six months he has been out twice. Once to see his physician about two months ago and once this week to go to the Royal House late at night."

I didn't bother to tell him that the second visit had been to me. "What about others?" I asked.

"We have been watching a number of suspects, but none of them have any contact with Rouen—with one exception."

"Eddie Capo," I said.

"Yes, Capo visits Rouen quite frequently. Rouen claims that he is interested in the reformation of Capo. I might add that we have not discovered any connection between Capo and the other suspects either. We have also checked every ship and the personnel of such ships and have not yet discovered how the narcotics are being brought in or by whom. But we do know that a large, steady supply is coming in through here and being distributed through New York."

"A leak?" I asked.

"Yes. There's been another bunch in New York trying to hijack their supply, and one of them talked."

"They're careless about life, trying to hijack the Syndicate," I said. "What about your other suspects?"

"What about them?"

"Can you tell me who they are?"

"No. If you want to guess, within reason, I'll tell you if you're right."

"Okay," I said. "I have only three names I want to know about. Adam Perrin?"

"The undertaker? Yes, he's one. But we haven't been able to get a thing on him. He's never gone near a ship or near any of the other suspects."

"Narcisse Coillon?"

He shook his head. "Nothing on him. He visits Rouen frequently, but it doesn't seem to have any connection. He is a relative of Rouen's and has occasionally received support from him."

"West Carroll?"

He frowned. "The name's familiar. Oh, yes, he was the boatman in that case you're working on, wasn't he? No, we have nothing pointing to him."

"What about Willie Morell?"

He shook his head. "That's four," he pointed out.

"I always have trouble counting," I said. "I guess that's all."

"All right, let me ask you a couple of questions. How did you get on to Rouen?"

"He and Capo got on to me," I said. "They seem to feel my

work on the murder of the two men may interfere with them."

"How's that?"

"I'm not sure. But my theory is that the two men stumbled onto something—perhaps some information—which they weren't even aware they had, and were killed for it. I'm willing to bet I'm right."

He gnawed on his upper lip. "Maybe. What made you ask about Perrin?"

"He's the one who tried to get rid of the bodies. He claims he was hired over the phone and paid with money slipped under the door. But it also occurred to me that he might be an ideal man to do a lot of dirty work just because he's so obvious."

"Meaning what?"

"The red hearse. It's practically a landmark, so who's going to pay any attention to it—except to make some remark about the color of it?"

He nodded. "Coillon?"

"No suspicion, but he guided my two men, so I wondered about him."

"Morell?"

"Same. He was the diviner."

"Carroll?"

"He was the boatman. That's all. And that makes seven questions you've asked, not just a couple."

"I can count," he said, grinning at me, "but I just don't give a damn. You know anything else?"

"No, but I expect to."

"You'll give it to us if you get anything?"

"Sure."

"First?" he said firmly.

"I can't guarantee that," I said. "I talk in my sleep. But you'll get it. Well, thanks. I'll see you around."

"Yes," he said thoughtfully. He was looking at my coat. "You always carry a gun, Mr. March?"

"Only when I'm dressed," I said gravely. "And I have a permit." I walked to the door and then I looked back at him. "By the way, I've seen that thoughtful look before. Don't put a tail on me. I don't like them and I'll only have to lose him."

He grinned at me and I walked out.

I got into my rented car and drove back to the hotel. It was a little before eleven. I told the operator that I'd be in the bar if a call came for me. I went into the bar and ordered a dry martini.

The call came in about twenty minutes. I took it on one of the house phones in the bar.

"Mr. March?" the voice said. "This is Willie. You wanted me to call about them spirits I was tellin' you about."

"Relax, Willie," I said. "If anybody's listening in on my phone calls, I'll refuse to pay my bill and I'll yell for the FBI." There was a slight click as the operator cut out. "Well, what do you know? She was listening in. All right, be yourself, Willie."

"Okay," he said. "I can be available whenever you want me."

"Good. Meet me here at the hotel in about an hour."

"Right," he said and hung up.

I had another martini, then went in to lunch. When I

finished lunch, I left word where I'd be and headed back for the bar. I had a Canadian Club and water and sipped it.

A bellboy came in looking for me a few minutes later. I beckoned and he came over.

"There's a nigra in the lobby asking for you, sir," he said.

"Oh?" I said. "Well, I'll go right out." I stood up and reached in my pocket while he waited expectantly. "Oh, by the way, I always tip according to how words are pronounced." I dropped a nickel into his hand. "Go have yourself a honeymoon. That'll get you into a little building that has a sign saying *Whites Only.*" I turned and walked away while he was still staring at the nickel.

Willie was waiting in the lobby, hat in hand, giving a good imitation of Uncle Tom in his younger years.

"Don't you dare call me Marse Milo," I said under my breath as I came up. "Look, Willie, I'm sorry. I didn't think or I wouldn't have told you to meet me here. Let's get the hell out of here."

We went out and walked down to where I'd parked the car. "We might as well get into the car and talk," I said. "Maybe I'll feel less like Simon Legree."

He laughed as we got into the car. "Dem bad spirits sho got you, suh," he said, putting it on thick.

"Yeah," I said. "The only kind of spirits that ever treat me kindly are those that come in bottles. ... Willie, I don't know what the hell I'm doing in this case, so I'm flying by the seat of my pants. I can use a little help, if you're willing. I'll pay you the same amount you charge for divining."

"Okay," he said. "What can I do?"

"I think I'll put you on the night shift. You know where a guy named Raoul Rouen lives?"

"I know where the Rouen mansion is. Everybody in New Orleans knows it."

"All right. Come back here tonight and take the car. Here's a duplicate set of keys. I'll leave it parked along here and you can just take it and then leave it here in the morning. I want you to find a place where you can watch Rouen's house— preferably the back. Any visitors that I'll be interested in will probably come and go that way. Think you can do that?"

"It'll be a cinch. There's another old mansion just back of his house that's been deserted for years. It's all overgrown. I used to play there when I was a kid. It's a perfect place for watching his house."

"There's one thing to be careful about," I said. "I think the FBI are also watching the house, so don't let them catch you. Now, I want you to follow anybody that visits him at night, except a guy named Eddie Capo. He's a little, tough-looking guy who will probably always arrive and leave in a black Cadillac. Ignore him. But follow anybody else that visits the house. You'll probably need the car for that. And as near as you can, remember and tell me everything the person does. Okay?"

"Okay!"

"You probably won't have to stay all night. Once all the lights in the house go out and everything seems quiet, you can probably knock off. Use your own judgment. I don't think the old man ever goes to bed very early. Whenever you knock off, bring the car back here and then call me sometime during the day. Don't try to do anything but watch, and don't get caught. If the cops stop you anytime, just tell them you've been hired to drive for me and I gave you the car to use that night. Got a girl?"

"Sort of. Nothing serious."

"If you're careful, this shouldn't be dangerous. If you want extra cover-up, take the girl along with you. But don't tell her what you're doing. Again, I leave it up to you. Anybody who can get away with that divining mumbo jumbo you do ought to be able to think his way through this. Okay, run along. I'll leave the car here sometime before it's dark. There's no point in starting to watch until after that."

"I'll see you," he said. He slipped out of the car and started down the street, automatically falling into a shambling gait. I watched him, thinking I had made a good choice. Nobody would ever think of him as doing the kind of work I was giving him.

I decided to take the afternoon off. Or to partly take it off. I wanted to talk to West Carroll more. One thing kept bothering me. He'd been on the boat that night, and sounds carry over the water. He should have heard something, even oarlocks if someone had been using a rowboat. I got out of the car and hunted up a store where I could buy a pair of swimming trunks. Then I got into the car and started for the docks.

I'd gone only about three blocks when I knew that someone was following me. But I wouldn't have to worry about losing him, so I grinned to myself and kept on going.

I parked near the docks and walked out on the pier. There were a few people strolling around, mostly tourists just looking. I stopped about halfway down the pier and pretended to examine one of the boats. In the meantime, I kept a watch on the way I had come. It wasn't hard to spot him even though he came along as though he was sightseeing. He was another college-type young man, so I guessed he came from the office I'd visited that morning. I turned and walked on down the pier.

West Carroll's boat was tied up at the dock and he was sitting on the deck, smoking a cigarette. He stared at me blankly as I stopped in front of him.

"Busy?" I asked.

"Do I look like it?" he countered.

I grinned. "Want to go skin diving?"

"You paying?"

"I'm paying," I said.

"Then let's go," he said.

I went aboard and he started the motor and cast off. As the boat backed away from the pier, I saw my tail standing with a bunch of tourists and looking baffled. I grinned at him and relaxed.

"How come you're not out looking for that killer?" Carroll asked. He'd turned the boat and we were already heading out, picking up speed.

"Let the cops do it," I said. "All work and no play makes jack. And if I got rich I'd have to sit around worrying about people wanting to take my money away from me. Then my girl's out of town, so I decided to have some fun."

He grunted.

"Where are we going?" I asked him.

"There's a place out in the Gulf," he said, "where I usually go. It's deep enough and the water's good and clear. There are usually plenty of fish around too if you like to try for them."

"With a spear?" I asked.

"Nah," he said. "That's too easy. Any kid can get them with a spear. Use a knife and it's more sporting."

"Whatever you say," I told him. "I'm game to try anything once."

"You said you've been skin diving before?"

"A few times. Not recently, though."

He grunted again and turned his attention to the boat. There was considerable traffic on the Mississippi, everything from big freighters to little outboard motorboats. We wove our way between them, Carroll handling the wheel in a manner that showed this was something that gave him pleasure.

Before long we were out in the wide sweep of the Gulf. He gave the boat full throttle; the stern settled down in the water as it picked up speed. We traveled for several more minutes, then he swung the boat in toward shore and cut the throttle. A moment later, he shut off the motor and dropped anchor.

"We're here," he said. "Get into your trunks."

We went into the cabin. I undressed and got into my swimming trunks. He tossed me a pair of flippers for my feet, a pair of goggles, and an air tank. In the meantime, he had stripped and was getting into his own gear.

"Here," he said. He tossed a knife on the bench beside me. It was a wicked-looking weapon with a blade fully eight inches long.

"Quite a sticker," I said.

"Yeah," he said. "It's good for getting fish. And if you get tangled up in any seaweed, you'll be damn glad you have it. Let's go."

We went out on the deck and he dropped over the side. I followed him and started swimming down. I could see him a few feet away, gliding down through the water with effortless strokes. He was good at it. The water was a clear green, and as I went lower I could see for sixty feet or more in every direction. Schools of fish darted past us.

He looked around and spotted me. He gestured with one hand and I swam toward him. When I reached him, he pointed ahead. I looked and there was a school of fairly large fish straight ahead. He touched my shoulder. I looked around and he motioned me to go after them.

Although I had done some diving, this was one aspect of it I had never tried. But I wasn't going to admit defeat without making an effort. I gripped my knife more firmly and swam ahead with as little motion as possible, but the fish scurried away while I was still twenty feet from them. I looked back at Carroll and shrugged. He had a disgusted expression on his face as he gestured for me to follow him.

We swam a few more feet and spotted another small school of fish. Some of these were quite large. Carroll motioned me to stay back and swam straight down. When he was considerably below them, he drifted slowly ahead until he was directly underneath them. He hung there for a moment, completely motionless, then suddenly shot upward. There was a flurry of movement and the water clouded. All I could see was Carroll's flippers as he continued up toward the surface. I kicked my flippers and went after him.

I surfaced only a minute after he did, in time to see him toss-
ing a fish onto the deck of the boat. It looked as if it weighed
a good seven or eight pounds.

"My dinner," he said. He put his mouthpiece back in his
mouth and his body jackknifed as he dived again. I stayed
on the surface for a minute, looking around. The Gulf was
calm, looking like a giant sheet of glass. Way off on the horizon a freighter made its way, balanced on what seemed to be
the rim of the world. Nearer, a launch cut the smooth water
as it curved somewhat in our direction. I turned and dived.

Carroll was down about twenty feet stalking another school
of fish. I decided not to try it again. I went on past him, down
to the floor of the Gulf. Seaweed floated lazily in the slight
undercurrent and tiny fish darted in every direction. The light
was weird and wonderful in this strange world, which had
fascinated me from the time I made my first dive. I drifted
slowly along just a couple of feet from the bottom, enjoying
myself. Prisms of light through the water made everything
dance and shimmer as though every image might break and
vanish any minute.

I don't know how long it was before I realized that everything was shimmering more than it should and that I was
gulping for air. I was running out of oxygen. I reached back
to turn on the five-minute reserve supply that every tank
has. I turned it on, but nothing happened. It was empty, too.
I turned and pushed myself frantically upward.

I don't know how far I had gone when I realized I wasn't
going to make it. My lungs felt as if they were on fire as I strug-

gled for air that didn't exist. My arms and legs felt too heavy to move. The water around me grew darker and darker, then I seemed to spin right into the blackness. …

TEN

As though from a great distance, I heard voices, but the words were garbled and hollow-sounding, as if they were coming through water. Something hard was pressing on my back. I struggled to get away from it and suddenly became aware that I was breathing. My first thought was that I had developed gills and was able to breathe under water. Then the words around me began to clear up and make sense.

"—something wrong with his oxygen gear," a voice near me said. There was something familiar about it.

"Lucky you saw there was something wrong," another voice said from farther away, "and pulled him out."

"Yeah," said the voice over me.

I opened my eyes. I was lying on the deck of the boat and West Carroll was kneeling beside me. I forced myself up on one elbow and looked around. There was another boat near us with two men on it. One of them was the young man who had been following me earlier, but at the moment I didn't even care. My head still felt too light for my body and my chest hurt, but I was alive. That was more than I expected not long before.

"You all right?" Carroll asked.

"I guess so," I said. I managed to sit up, shaking my head to clear it.

"Had a narrow one, eh?" the other boatman called. "It's a good thing West saw there was something wrong. Got you out just in time, it looked like."

I looked at Carroll. "You pulled me out?"

"Yeah. I was up on the surface and just started to dive when I saw you floating up. I grabbed you and got you aboard. I wasn't sure you were going to make it then, but pretty soon you started quivering like a pair of frog legs in a skillet, so I knew you were okay."

"Thanks," I said.

"Just part of the service," he said, shrugging.

"What happened?" I asked.

"It was my fault," he said. "You got an oxygen tank that hadn't been serviced. So you didn't have enough oxygen. Even the reserve was empty. I serviced the tanks this morning, but I must have missed one. Sorry."

"Looks like you made up for it," I said. I climbed unsteadily to my feet. "But I guess I've had it for today. Let's go back."

"Sure," he said. He helped me into the cabin and I slowly began to dress. He dressed more quickly and went out and started the motor. He pulled up the anchor and we got under way. I looked out and saw the other boat moving, too, trying to look as if it weren't following us. My little Federal pal was determined to keep me in sight.

After I was dressed, I stayed in the cabin, resting. I still felt exhausted.

When we finally docked, I paid Carroll and thanked him again. Then I got into the Cadillac and drove back to the hotel. My friend was still behind me, but I didn't care.

I parked the car near the hotel and went in, heading straight for the bar. A couple of drinks later I was feeling a little better, although my chest still ached. But my head was certainly better and once more able to produce thoughts. I didn't like what I was thinking.

West Carroll admitted that he'd given me the wrong oxygen tank by accident. Only I didn't really believe in accidents. I supposed it was possible to forget to service a tank, but why did I get it instead of some giggling matron from Keokuk? Why had it happened so soon after Rouen had threatened to have me killed and when I was alone with a man who had been along when the other two men were killed? Accident or not, it had almost fulfilled the threat. It probably would have made no difference if I hadn't been so far down.

True, Carroll had pulled me out and saved my life. But, I told myself, that could have been because he discovered there was another boat near enough to see what was going on. Maybe I was being unduly suspicious, but I decided I was going to be even more interested in West Carroll in the future.

I had another drink and went upstairs to take a nap. I needed to recover fully before I tried anything else. I had barely stretched out on the bed when the phone rang. I picked up the receiver and said hello. It was New York calling. I waited a minute and then Martin Raymond came on.

"Milo," he said, "I see where they've found the bodies of those two men." He didn't sound very happy about it.

"I found them," I said. "So we can rule out the idea that they were pulling a fraud."

"This is the fourth day you've been down there," he said. "What have you got?"

"Not very much," I admitted.

"What about Lane?" he asked.

"He's still around—by request of the police. Frankly, I don't think he did it, but we won't know for sure until we know who did do it."

"I don't like spending so much money on this," he complained. "Especially if Lane isn't guilty. We'll be stuck for a hundred and fifty thousand dollars plus your fee and expenses. Can't you hurry it up a little?"

"Look," I said. "I've been here for three and a half days. I've been tramping over a lousy little island filled with quicksand pits. I've been threatened three times by a guy who was a triggerman for Murder, Inc. I've also been told by one of the top men of the Crime Syndicate that he will have me killed. And I've just barely escaped from dying out in the middle of the Gulf. All this for a lousy hundred bucks a day. What do you want—blood?"

"I don't understand," he said. "It's just a simple little insurance case."

"Sure," I said. "That's what I thought, too. A simple little case. It's getting so damned complicated that any minute I expect to hear that Russia is going to declare war if I solve it."

"But—but why? Do you mean those two men were mixed up in something criminal?" There was a faint note of hope in his voice.

"No," I said. "Or at least, I don't think so. I think maybe they did stumble on something and were killed for that. But it's getting pretty clear that nobody wants it solved except the city and Federal cops—and sometimes it seems to me that they're a minority."

"Well, if it's going to be too dangerous … ," he began.

"Nuts," I told him. "You won't be sure until Lane is proved innocent or guilty. Even if you're going for the hundred and fifty grand, you might as well go for another few hundred and know that you weren't taken. Just take a tranquilizer and relax."

"Well, all right. But try to speed it up."

"Yes, sir," I said. "Speed it up. I just made a note of that." I banged the receiver back on the hook. Then I remembered that I had wanted to make a phone call. I picked it up again and gave the operator Lieutenant Stern's number.

"Get anything from the bag yet?" I asked when he answered.

"Yes. It was human blood, all right, so you probably found the place they were killed. What's with you? I've been sitting here waiting for you to bring in the killer."

"I took the afternoon off," I said. "Went skin diving."

"How was it?"

"Wet." I told him. I wasn't going to tell him any more. Even if my suspicions were right, I'd handle it my own way. "Another thing, Lieutenant. When you recovered those bodies, did you find the treasure map on either one of them?"

"No. If one of them had it, maybe it went the same place their money went."

"You mean they had been robbed, too?"

"Yeah. Lane didn't know how much they were carrying but guessed that they had two or three hundred dollars between them. But it was gone. We questioned Perrin, but he swore he didn't take anything out of their pockets."

"Okay," I said. "You take care of the store. I'm going to sleep." I hung up and did so.

It wasn't much of a sleep, because I kept dreaming that I was drowning, and I finally awakened drenched in sweat. I got up and took a shower and felt a little better. Then I shaved and went downstairs. I was still feeling shaky.

Peter Lane was in the bar and the redhead was with him. He was certainly picking the nicest way to forget his sorrows. I went over and joined them.

"Well, if it isn't my two oldest friends," I said. I peered at the redhead. "Where is it that I don't remember you from? Oh, yes, Paris. Look, honey, I want to talk to your boyfriend for just a minute. Why don't you run off to the powder room and powder your nose. Say about ten minutes?"

She made a face at me and left.

"Something up?" Lane asked anxiously as soon as she was gone.

"Nothing serious," I said. "You guys had a map of Placide Island, didn't you?"

"Yes."

"Who has it now?"

"Why, I don't know," he said. "Oh, I remember. Herman was carrying it that night, so the police must have it."

"Uh-uh," I said.

"You mean that may be the reason they were killed?"

"I don't mean anything of the kind. I suppose it's possible, but I don't believe it. But I was just curious about where it was. Okay, thanks, Lane. Have fun." I walked down to the other end of the bar and ordered a martini. While I was sipping it, the redhead came back and joined Lane. I blew her a kiss when she looked my way.

Later I went into the dining room and had dinner. After that I returned to the bar and brooded over a number of drinks. When I finally had a comfortable glow, I went upstairs and went to bed early. Before I turned in, I took one peek through the curtains at the apartment across the street. There was no sign of life in it. Ever since that night when I discovered Eddie Capo had taken it, I'd been keeping the curtains closed, although it was possible that it had been taken for just that one night so he could cover Rouen while he visited me.

I was awakened the next morning by the phone. I fumbled for the receiver and mumbled something into it.

"Good morning, darling," she said. It was Lisette. "Did I wake you up?"

"Yeah."

"I'm sorry."

"Don't be," I told her. "Only I wish you wouldn't do it by phone. A telephone is only frustrating for the sort of ideas I get when you wake me up."

She laughed. "I'm sorry I awakened you, darling, but I just got back and I thought perhaps you would meet me for breakfast."

"Of course," I said. "Where?"

"The Morning Call?"

"Okay."

"I'm still at the airport," she said, "so why don't you plan on meeting me there in about forty-five minutes?"

"Okay, honey," I said. "I'll be there."

I hung up and jumped out of bed. A good night's sleep seemed to have done the job for me. I felt fine. I went in and took a shower and got dressed. I went downstairs and found the car parked not far from the hotel. I got in and drove toward the French Quarter. I parked about a block from the restaurant and got out. I checked the door to see if it was locked.

"Good morning, Mr. March," a voice said.

I looked around. It was Narcisse Coillon. I wondered what he was doing there, but then I remembered he lived not far away.

"Good morning," I said. "Not working today?"

"Yes. Just going to see a client. You still worrying about the two men, Mr. March?"

"In a way," I said.

"You'll find the treasure is at the bottom of it," he said cheerfully. "People will do anything when there is a treasure to be found. Well, if you need me again, Mr. March ..."

"Sure," I said. I went on down to the restaurant and found Lisette already there, sitting at one of the little tables in the back. I leaned over and kissed her, then sat down.

"How was the trip?" I asked.

"Fine," she said. "Did you miss me?"

"Terribly," I said.

The waiter came back. "You left your cigarettes at the counter, Miss Dufresne," he said, putting them down in front of her.

"Thank you, John," she said. "I got here quicker than I expected and had a cup of coffee at the counter while I was waiting for you," she added to me.

We ordered and the food was soon brought. We talked about trivialities while we ate, but even that was fun.

"And what's been happening with you?" she asked as we started on our coffee.

"Practically nothing," I admitted.

"No solution to the case yet?"

"No."

"That's good," she said with a smile. "It means you'll stay here longer."

"Not too much longer, baby," I said. "The company's going to get tired of paying me if nothing happens. But maybe something will break soon."

"You have an idea?"

"I have lots of those, but they haven't done me any good yet."

"You'll do it, darling."

"Maybe. What'll we do tonight?"

"I don't know. There's a lot of New Orleans you haven't seen yet. I'll think of something."

When we had finished our coffee, I drove her home. On the way back to the hotel, I had an idea. I stopped off and called the Federal office I had visited the day before. "This is Milo March," I said when the man answered.

"Oh, yes, Mr. March. I understand that you almost had an accident yesterday."

"Yeah," I said. "Tell that beagle of yours that the first time it's important I'll leave him standing on the corner. Is he with me this morning? I haven't bothered to look."

"Probably."

"Well, all he can tell you is that I went to have breakfast with a young lady."

"Was it an accident yesterday?" he asked.

"Sure," I said. "I want to ask you something. You have any idea at all where the drugs are coming from that are being brought in here?"

"We know where they're coming from," he said. "They're coming from Italy. You know they have a good connection over there. What we want to know is how they're brought in. We've checked every ship sailing from Italy in the past year—there and here both."

"And no dice, huh?"

"No. We do know that it's coming in at this port and then sent on to New York. We just got more confirmation of this. The New York police have picked up a man who's part of the group that's been trying to cut in on it. He's a fourth offender, so he's talking. Doesn't know much, but he also knows that it's all coming from here. Mostly heroin. You uncovered anything?"

"No," I said. "I'll let you know when I do." I hung up and went back and sat in the car awhile. I was getting a sort of idea. It wasn't much—maybe no more than that I was suspicious and angry. I went back to the drugstore and looked up the address of the main public library. I went back to the car and drove to it.

I went in and got copies of the leading newspaper for every

day during the past three weeks. I carried them over to one of the tables and started going through them. But all I was interested in was the shipping news. I went through the lists, looking only for ships that had sailed from Italian ports for New Orleans. The first one I found was for two weeks and five days earlier—the night that the two men had been killed. A ship, coming from Italy, had been due in New Orleans that night at nine-thirty. When I turned to the next day's paper, I learned that the ship had actually docked an hour late.

The next one that had come in from Italy had been the night I went out to look at Placide Island. There were no more listed. I took the papers back to the desk and left, feeling that for the first time maybe I was on to something. I didn't quite know how or what, but I had a hunch that I had the first lead.

I drove back to the hotel and parked. I went inside, picking up a newspaper from the cigar stand, left word where I'd be, and went into the bar. I was becoming almost as much a fixture there as the stools. The bartender looked at me, glanced at the clock, and saw it was getting near to noon, so he started mixing a martini without waiting to be told. I grinned at him to prove that I recognized a sterling character when I saw one.

The paper had a follow-up story on the murder of the two men from New York, but it didn't contain anything I didn't already know. I turned back to the shipping news and saw what I was looking for. There was another freighter due in from Italy the next night. Docking at five o'clock in the morning. That would give me a chance to prove whether I was right.

I was idly reading the rest of the paper and sipping my martini when a bellboy came in to tell me that there was a phone call for me and I could take it on the extension in the bar. I flipped a quarter to him and went over to the extension.

"Milo March," I told the operator. "You have a call for me. Only this time don't try listening in, honey."

"Well!" she exclaimed. She connected me and shut off her key with a bang that I couldn't help hearing. "Hello," I said.

"This is Willie," he said.

"Hi," I said. "Did you have any luck last night?"

"Some, I think," he said. "But I'm not sure I should tell it to you over the phone. Should I?"

"Maybe you're right. Where are you, Willie?"

"About three blocks from your hotel."

"Then meet me at the car. It's parked about a half a block from where you left it this morning, on the same street."

"Okay," he said.

I hung up and went back and finished my drink. The bartender was about to start another one but I shook my head. "I'll be back," I told him as I paid him. I went out and walked up to the car. I unlocked it and got in to wait. I looked around and saw the nice young Federal man sitting in his car across the street pretending to read a newspaper. He'd only amused me before, but for some reason it annoyed me this time.

Willie came along a minute later. He opened the door and slid in beside me.

"Hold it a minute, Willie," I said. "We're going to have some fun."

I put the key in and started the motor. I pulled out into the street, driving slowly. Watching in the rearview mirror, I saw the Federal man pull out and follow. By the time we reached the next block he was right behind me. I swerved quickly to the curb and stopped. I had caught him by surprise and there was nothing he could do but drive past me. I pulled out again immediately right behind him.

"What's going on?" Willie asked.

"That guy's been following me for two days," I said. "Now I'm following him and he doesn't know what to do."

He didn't, either. He tried going real slow, hoping that I'd pass him. I didn't, but stuck right behind him. Finally, he speeded up and so did I. But just then he passed an intersection and I swung quickly into it, pushing the accelerator to the floor. The Cadillac jumped as if somebody had put a torch to its rear fenders. I turned again at the next intersection and raced back the four blocks we had come. Two more turns and I was back on the street where the hotel was. I parked in the same spot we'd been in before.

"He'll wander around for a few minutes before he figures out what may have happened to him," I said, grinning. "That ought to teach him to respect his betters. Okay, Willie, what happened?"

"Well," he said, "I went up to watch the house about nine o'clock. Nothing happened until about eleven when that black Cadillac came. The guy you described got out and went inside. He was still there later when I left. Then about midnight Coillon arrived. He came the back way, passing within a few feet of where I was hiding. He was inside maybe thirty minutes. When he left, I followed him. I was lucky, too. He'd parked his old car about a block ahead of where I had your car parked. I followed him and he drove down to the docks. He parked and got into that outboard motorboat he keeps down there and took off. I didn't have any way of following him over the water, so I just sat down there to wait."

"Good work," I said.

"I guess he was gone almost an hour and then he came back and docked. When he got out of the boat he was carrying something in a gunnysack. I don't know what it was, but it was pretty bulky. He got into his car and drove away. I followed. You know where he went?"

"No," I said, "but nothing is going to surprise me."

"There's an alley that runs the length of one block behind Perdido Street. He turned into that alley and switched his lights off. I knew I couldn't follow him into the alley, so I ran past it and parked. Then I walked back to watch. He'd stopped just behind the undertaker's. He got out and there was enough light so I could see that he had the gunnysack with him. He wasn't gone more than a minute, but when he came back he didn't have the sack. What do you suppose was in there? It wasn't big enough to be a body—unless it was a child."

"In a way, it was maybe a lot of bodies," I said. "What then?"

"He just went home. I drove back up to the Rouen house, but the Cadillac was gone and the lights were out, so I went home. But that isn't all."

"What else?"

"I didn't get a chance to see Coillon yesterday to tell him

that I wouldn't be able to work with him in the next few days, so I went over to see him early this morning. When I got there he was just leaving his house."

"What time?" I asked.

"It was about nine-thirty."

"I saw him about nine," I said, "and he said he was going to meet a client."

"That's what he told me at nine-thirty when I met him coming out of the house," Willie said. "Anyway, I told him I was working for the next few days, tipped my hat, and left. But when I got to the corner I got a taxi and followed him. His car was still in sight."

"Willie, you're a gem," I said. "I'll return the taxi money to you."

"Well, anyway, he went back up to the Rouen house again. This time he wasn't inside more than fifteen or twenty minutes, then came back. I'd let the taxi go, so I didn't follow him when he drove away. There wasn't another cab around."

"It's all right," I said. "He probably wasn't going anywhere else that was important in the daytime. You did fine. In fact, you did better than fine."

"Great," he said with a grin, "but what does it all mean?"

"I'll be honest with you, Willie," I said. "I'm not sure that I know myself. I'm just sort of guessing and making some wild jumps. But if I'm right, your friend Coillon picked up some drugs somewhere and delivered them to the undertaker. Now the next question is what is the undertaker going to do with them?"

"I could go watch him tonight," Willie said.

"I'd been thinking about that," I said. "I don't know. Night may not be the time to watch him. He may make his delivery in the day. Normally nobody pays any attention to a hearse. In the case of his red hearse, people pay so much attention to it that they don't think of it as anything except a peculiar hearse."

"I could watch him today."

"It may be too late already," I said. "It's a quarter to twelve. Did you get any sleep?"

"All I need," he said.

"All right," I said suddenly. "Take the car and make a stab at it. But be careful. I think the cops may be watching Perrin, too, so don't let them catch you."

"I won't," he said. I looked at him. He was enjoying himself.

"Relax," I told him. "There's no future in it. Okay. Let me know what happens." I got out of the car and he slid under the wheel. I slammed the door and waved to him as he pulled out. I started back for the hotel and just then I saw the Federal man come driving back down the street. When I was sure that he saw me, I blew a kiss to him.

I reached the hotel and was about to go in when I had an idea. I crossed the street to the apartment house and rang the superintendent's bell. The same little old lady came to the door, only this time her hair wasn't in curlers.

"Is the front apartment on the third floor still rented?" I asked.

She peered at me. "Oh, you're the gentleman who inquired the day after it was rented," she said. "How lucky that you thought of coming back. The gentleman who rented it came back a couple of days later and said he'd changed his mind, but I could keep the rent he'd given me. So it is vacant. Would you like to see it?"

"Not just now," I said. "I'm not quite sure yet whether I'll be able to take it or not. I'll come back and let you know."

"Well, my goodness, you were so anxious," she said.

"I'm like that," I told her. I winked. "Fits, you know." I turned and went back to the hotel. The bartender saw me coming and started stirring up my second martini. A good man.

After lunch I bought a couple of magazines and went up to my room. I still had part of a bottle of Canadian Club left, so I phoned down and had room service send up some ice. I took off my shoes and stretched out on the bed.

It was almost six o'clock when my phone call finally came. It was Willie.

"I'm about a block from the hotel," he said. "You want to meet me and I'll tell you what happened?"

"I'll be right down," I said. I put the receiver back. Then I got my shoes and coat on and went downstairs. I found the car parked, with Willie in it, about a block away, as he'd said. I got in next to him.

"I don't really know if anything happened or not," he said. "The red hearse was still parked in front of the funeral parlor when I got there. He came out and got into it maybe a half hour later. And you were right about him being followed. I let the cop follow him first, then I followed the cop. We made a regular damn parade, but if the undertaker was aware of it, he didn't let on. In the next two hours he made fifteen stops.

None of them took long and none of them seemed important. I have all the addresses here." He took out a slip of paper and gave it to me. I looked at it, but none of the addresses meant anything to me.

"No bulky gunnysack this time?" I asked.

"No. He wasn't carrying anything that could be seen when he went into any of the places or when he came out. You know, too, he seemed to be enjoying himself. Once I even had the thought that he knew he was being followed and was doing this just to bother whoever was following him."

"Could be," I said. "If he has any brains at all, he must know the cops are keeping an eye on him."

"Anyway, after that he went back to the funeral parlor. About half an hour later, there was a funeral service there. Maybe about a dozen people came. Then they carried a coffin out to the hearse and he drove to the cemetery with it. The family went along. Then back to the funeral parlor, and I guess he's still there. But the first part is screwy."

"Yeah," I said. I was thinking about it. "You know, if I'm right about what Coillon delivered there last night, it was probably in some kind of container. The heroin itself wouldn't be so bulky. Five or ten pounds of pure heroin is worth a hell of a lot of money. And if I'm right, he could probably take the heroin out of the container and carry it on his person without its showing. As I said, he must know the cops are watching him, so he wouldn't want to keep the heroin around the funeral parlor any longer than necessary. So he must have made a drop today. One of the fifteen stops might have been for that and the other fourteen were just to throw off anyone following him. What kind of places were these? Residences or shops?"

He thought a minute. "Three of them were shops, one was a department store, and the others were apartment houses."

"And no way of telling which apartment he went into—if any," I said. "Unless they stop him and search him, he's safe doing it even with the cops following him—and they aren't following him because they suspect him of carrying drugs. But, again if I'm right, he probably wouldn't want to keep the container around long either. But what the hell would he do with it? Throw it out in the garbage?"

"I don't think so," Willie said. "When I went there today, I drove through that alley just out of curiosity. There wasn't anything to see. But I remember his garbage cans were out, and I don't think there was anything there but garbage. And that gunnysack last night was pretty bulky."

"No, he wouldn't do that either," I said. I was really talking to myself. "If the narcotics were in a container, it was probably whatever container was used to smuggle the stuff into the country, and so it might attract too much attention. But how the hell would you get rid of the thing?"

"I know how maybe he might get rid of that one," Willie said.

"How?"

"Well, he had a funeral today. After the relatives got through looking at the remains, why couldn't he put it in the coffin just before he closed it?"

I stared at him. "Willie," I said slowly, "I have a feeling that you're a genius. It's certainly worth checking on."

"How can we?"

"You keep the car," I said, "and meet me back here about one o'clock tonight. You and I are going to do a little grave robbing."

ELEVEN

He stared at me for a minute after I'd spoken, then he suddenly grinned, shaking his head.

"Boss," he said, going back to that other voice he used, "you is as nervy as a gnat. Not only is you goin' into a cemetery in the middle of the night, but you is planning on takin' a burr-head with you. Man, you is a real hickory-nut cracker."

"I'm not a cracker," I said, "I'm a Yankee. But drop the vaudeville bit. On the other hand, I'm aware that it's probably some kind of felony and you don't have to come if you don't want to."

"I wouldn't miss it for the world," he said. "I've got to have something to tell my grandchildren when I'm an old man. I'll be here."

"Okay," I said. "What's the cemetery?"

"Saint Roch's Campo Santo."

"Will there be any sort of night watchman around?"

"I don't think so. But there'll be a big iron-grille gate, padlocked."

"Nothing," I said. "What'll we need? A flashlight, shovels—"

"No shovels," he said. "This was a poor family, so the coffin will be in one of the ovens."

"Ovens?" I asked.

"Yes. In the old days nobody was buried underground in New Orleans. The rich had tombs, of course. But the cemeteries were built with thick walls around them, in which there were niches or crypts where the poor were buried. They are still used. You can buy one of the ovens or rent one. In the latter case, if you don't keep up the rent, they take the body out and cremate it, so they can rent the oven to someone else."

"You mean," I asked, "that in New Orleans you can still get a dispossess notice after you're dead? What won't they think of next? Oh, well. You get whatever you think we'll need and meet me here at one o'clock. I don't know if my shadow will still be around, so park around the corner on the next block and I'll meet you there."

He nodded. I opened the door and got out. I went back to the hotel, shaved and changed clothes, then took a taxi to Lisette's. The Federal man, or maybe it was another one, faithfully followed the cab.

Lisette and I went out on the town again. No matter what we did, it was fun. She was beginning to be a habit with me. It was a long time since I'd had as much fun with any girl.

Shortly after midnight I told her that I had to go to work and I took her home. She was curious, but I didn't tell her anything. I figured if she knew, it would merely make her worry. I kissed her at the door and went straight back to the hotel.

Up in my room, I got out my suitcase and opened it. It had one special feature. The lining on the bottom of it could be lifted up if you knew how. I lifted it and took out a set of delicate steel picks, guaranteed to open any lock in the world if you knew how to use them.

I had gotten them in one of those Caribbean banana republics on my last case.* I put them in my pocket. I went back downstairs and hunted up a bellboy. I took five dollars from my pocket and folded it so that the five still showed.

"I have a phobia," I said. "You know what that is?"

"Yes, sir," he said. For five dollars he was going to know even if he had never heard of it before.

"As soon as it's midnight or after," I said gravely, "I don't like to go out the front door. Do you think maybe I could leave by the delivery entrance?"

"I'm sure you could, sir," the boy said. "I'll show you the way."

"I predict a great future for you, my boy," I said. I gave him the five dollars and followed him back through the kitchen to the delivery door. He held it open.

"Good night, sir," he said with a grin.

"Good night," I said. "By the way, if anyone should ask you, you haven't seen me."

"Of course not, sir," he said promptly. "I just came back for a breath of fresh air and haven't seen anyone."

"What's your name?" I asked him.

"Jack, sir."

"Okay, Jack. I'll remember it in case I have any petty crimes I want committed." I went out, walked a few steps, and found myself on the side street. The Cadillac was parked a few feet away. I opened the door and slipped in. "Let's go, Willie," I said.

---

* See *The Gallows Garden* by M.E. Chaber.

He started the motor, made a U-turn, and we sped away from the hotel. I checked through the rear window and no one was following us.

"What did you bring, Willie?" I asked.

"Flashlight and a small crowbar."

"Why a crowbar?"

"We may need it to pry open the coffin lid. And it could be used to break the chain on the gate."

"We won't need it for that."

We rode another fifteen minutes, then Willie pulled into the curb and stopped.

About a block ahead I could see a walled section. Within, a medieval-looking building reared against the sky. The street was deserted.

"This is it," Willie said, cutting the motor and the lights. "I did a little checking this evening. There isn't any night watchman. The sexton lives in a little building at the back of the cemetery. He's also quite old and deaf."

"What's that?" I asked, pointing to the building I could see.

"The chapel. It's fairly famous for healing. New Orleans girls also come to it to pray for husbands. Inside the chapel there is a statue of a child, but there are a lot of people in New Orleans who will swear to you that it's not a statue but the petrified body of the first child buried here."

"A tasty thought," I said. "You think we might have a better chance of success if we stopped and paid our respects to Saint Roch?"

"We might," he said. "Around here it is believed that Saint Roch is one of the eccentric saints like Saint Anthony. There are many pious people in New Orleans who believe that Saint Anthony has to be treated roughly. They will end a prayer to him by threatening to kick him in the pants if he doesn't grant their wish."

"A practical approach," I observed. "Let's go."

We got out of the car, Willie carrying the flashlight and the crowbar, and walked down to the gate. The street and sidewalk were deserted. I took out the picks and went to work on the padlock. It was a cinch. In about two minutes or less, it snapped open.

"You're pretty handy yourself," Willie said, lowering his voice.

I swung the gate open and we stepped inside. I closed the gate and fixed the chain and padlock so it would look as if it were locked.

"It'll be somewhere in the wall on the right," Willie said. "I could see that much this afternoon. We'll just have to look until we find a new coffin."

There was enough starlight for us to see as we circled around to the right, so we didn't use the flashlight until we reached the wall he'd mentioned. Willie cupped his hand around the flashlight so it wouldn't throw too much light, and we went down along the wall looking at the vaults. The wall was full of them, looking like a grim honeycomb.

We found it about halfway down, next to a chapel-like niche. I was glad to see that there was enough room in the vault for the coffin lid to be raised. I took the crowbar from Willie and pried the lid open. I lifted it and Willie flashed the light inside.

There was a little old man in the coffin, lying peacefully on his back. There certainly wasn't much danger of his getting up even if he came to life; there was a big chunk of steel resting on his chest. It was about three feet long and shaped like a torpedo.

"Willie, I love you," I said. I reached in and rolled the torpedo over. There were three bands around it with clamps on the underside. I handed the crowbar to Willie and used two hands to unscrew the head. Inside there was just hollow, empty space. I screwed the head back on and let the lid down.

"Let's go," I said. We made our way back to the gate and checked the street. There was no one in sight. We went out and I snapped the padlock shut. Then we walked quickly back to the car. Willie started the motor and we got under way.

"Why didn't you take it with you?" Willie asked.

"I want it there for evidence," I said. "We'll let the police find it later."

"What is it?" he asked.

"Well," I said, "back in the second World War it was a mine used to blow up ships. Now, stripped of its mechanism, I suspect it's a container for heroin. Or was."

We drove back to a block away from the hotel. "You take the car," I told Willie. "I don't suppose it'll turn up anything else, but you might as well cover our friend with the red hearse again. I'll need the car tomorrow night, so bring it around sometime in the evening."

"Okay," he said.

I got out of the car. It was two-thirty in the morning. I walked down the street, wondering if someone was still covering the hotel to see if I left. Someone was. I spotted him just as I reached the hotel. He was across the street in a parked car. I couldn't see what he looked like, but I could see his outlines and the glow of his cigarette. When I was sure he had seen me, I grinned at him and went into the hotel. When I got upstairs I went right to sleep.

I slept late the next morning. Then I got up and leisurely showered and shaved. I went downstairs, picked up a morning paper, and went into the coffee shop. I looked at the shipping news first. The SS *Maria* was still due to dock in New Orleans at five the next morning.

After breakfast I went out and sat in the lobby while I finished reading the paper. Then I went to a phone booth and called Lieutenant Stern.

"What's new?" I asked.

"Nothing," he said sourly. "We're still working, if that's what you mean. On your case and four others. What have you been doing?"

"Just taking it easy," I said, "and thinking."

"Better watch that, boy. It'll get you nowhere. How are you getting along with your friend Eddie Capo?"

"Haven't seen him recently. I guess he's just the fickle type. What time do you get to work these days, Lieutenant?"

"Seven in the morning. Why?"

"What do I do if I want to get you when you're not on duty?"

"You people think a cop is supposed to work twenty-four hours a day," he groaned. But he gave me his home phone number. "You on the trail of something?"

"No," I said. "It's just that I can't sleep sometimes at nights and I may want to talk to somebody."

"You keep this up," he said, "and I won't need a telegram from the New York cops in order to throw you in the pokey."

"On what charge?"

"Withholding evidence, interfering with the duty of an officer, loitering, and having no visible means of support. If that won't keep you on ice, I'll think of something else."

"Cops," I said. "Now, if you'll excuse me, I'll go wash my mouth out with soap. I'll see you around, Lieutenant." I hung up.

I made the most of the day off I was giving myself. I did a normal amount of tippling in the bar, had lunch in the dining room, and took a nap in the middle of the afternoon. That's the way I like to work. Besides, I expected to be up most of the night proving my theory.

Willie called a few minutes past five. "Nothing happened today," he said. "He only went out once, and that was to go to the store. Where do you want me to leave the car?"

"Don't bring it here," I said. I gave him Lisette's address on Royal Street. "Park it on the first side street below there. Far enough down the side street so it can't be seen from Royal Street unless you're right at the intersection."

"Right," he said. "You don't want me to watch the Rouen house tonight?"

"No. And I don't know what the schedule will be tomorrow. Tonight may tell the story. Call me during the day tomorrow. If you don't get me at first, keep trying."

"Okay," he said.

About an hour later I took a cab to Lisette's. I had just gotten out when I realized that one of the places Adam Perrin had stopped at the day before had been on Royal Street only a couple of blocks from where Lisette lived. I was a little early, so I decided to walk down and look at it. I did so, but it was a waste of time. It was an apartment building. There were twelve apartments in it, all of them occupied. I looked at the mailboxes, but there was no familiar name on them. Even if this was the drop, the odds were against my knowing which apartment he'd gone to. Rouen probably had a large organization.

As I was going back, I passed the Federal man, who was strolling down the opposite side of the street. He was not the one I'd seen before, but he was cut from the same cloth, so I had no doubt about who he was. I went on to Lisette's without looking back. She was ready and we went out to dinner. This time we went to the Court of Two Sisters for a quiet dinner by candlelight.

"I'm sorry, honey," I told her, "but I'm going to have to leave you early again tonight. More work."

"All right," she said. "I don't like it, but what can I do?" That was one of the things I liked about her; she didn't waste any time pouting or making a fuss.

"Maybe this'll be the last time, and then we can really celebrate," I said.

"You mean you've got it solved?" she asked excitedly.

"Maybe," I said. "Anyway, I think I'm going to catch a killer tonight."

She looked startled. "You will be careful, won't you, Milo?"

"I'm always careful," I told her.

"Want to tell me about it?" she asked.

"Not now. After it's all over. But I do think I know who killed the two men and why, and I may be able to prove part of it tonight. Now let's talk about something else."

So we did. And after dinner we went to the Roosevelt again and danced until it was time to take her home. I got her back to her apartment at twelve-thirty, with the Federal man still following faithfully. I went upstairs with her.

"Is there a back way out of here, honey?" I asked her.

"Yes," she said. "Just go down the back stairs and into the courtyard. There's a gate at the back of the courtyard and then a little graveled walk that leads to the street back of us. Why?"

"There's a little character who's been following me for the past several days, and I'd rather he didn't see me leave here. Of course, it may compromise you …"

"I wouldn't mind," she said smiling, "except that I don't get any of the advantages of it."

"There'll come a time," I said. I kissed her and went quickly down the back stairs. I went through the courtyard and was soon out on the other street. I turned to the left and walked down to the side street. I soon found the Cadillac where Willie had left it. I got in and drove away.

I thought that I had plenty of time, but I wanted to be sure, so I was giving myself an extra two or three hours. I drove down to the docks and cruised slowly along the street that ran beside the pier. There was a long line of still, dark boats bobbing gently at their moorings. The pier was deserted except for a small knot of men in front of one of the boats. There was enough light so that I could see that one of the men was West Carroll. That meant that I couldn't approach along the pier.

I drove on just past the end of the dock and parked around the corner, out of sight of the men. I quickly took off my clothes and put on my swimming trunks. I fastened the car keys to the waist of the trunks. Then I took a small waterproof bag that I had secured just in case it was needed and put my gun in it. I tied the bag around my neck. I left the car, ran back, and slipped into the water. I began swimming down behind the boats. Finally I reached Carroll's boat. I swam in beside it, on the far side from where the men were talking. They were maybe thirty feet away. I could hear the rumble of their voices, but couldn't make out the words.

On my third leap upward I managed to grab the edge of the deck. I pulled myself up until I could hook my elbows over the deck. Then I hung there until the warm wind pretty well dried me. When I felt sure that I wouldn't leave any wet tracks, I pulled myself up onto the deck and slipped quickly into the cabin. There was a long bench on one side which also served as a storage space for bedding and odds and ends. I opened the top and slipped inside. There was just enough room for me to lie there and close the lid. Since I was lying on blankets, it was very comfortable. The lid fit loosely enough to permit air inside.

I relaxed and prepared for a long wait. The only trouble was that I was almost too comfortable; I had to watch to be sure I didn't fall asleep. Once Carroll was aboard, even the slightest snore would give me away.

I don't know how long it was before I heard Carroll come aboard, but it must have been two hours, maybe longer. He came on whistling and puttered around in the cabin for a while. There was no way of telling what he was doing. Then, a bit later, the motor started and I could feel the boat moving away from the dock. Then the movement was reversed and we got under way, quickly picking up speed.

Again there was a long wait. How long I couldn't tell, but it was long enough to make me certain I was right. Finally, I could feel the slackening of speed, and then it seemed that the boat had stopped. I heard Carroll come into the cabin again, then leave. There was a peculiar slapping to the sound of his footsteps. I took the chance and raised the lid enough to give me a narrow peephole. I saw Carroll, in full skin-diving equipment, going over the side of the boat. I raised the lid farther and then I saw the freighter about twenty feet away moving slowly past the boat.

There were no lights on the boat, so I slipped out of the storage space and went to the window in the cabin. The moon was in its second quarter, and there was a dim light shed over the water. Carroll was nowhere in sight.

I stayed at the window, watching. When the freighter was already some fifteen feet past the boat, I saw Carroll's head suddenly break water. He turned on his back and began swimming toward the boat. He was carrying something cradled in his arms. The moonlight reflected from it.

I got back into the storage space and closed the lid. A few minutes later I heard Carroll dump something heavy on the floor. He went out and the motor roared as we got under way.

Going back took even longer, as near as I could estimate. But at long last I felt the boat slow up and finally stop. Once again Carroll entered the cabin and left. I could guess that he had come for the heavy object he'd left there. I waited a few minutes and risked raising the lid again. He wasn't on the boat. I raised it farther to make certain, then climbed out. I caught a brief glimpse of him wading ashore in the waning moonlight. He was still wearing the skin-diving equipment, with the goggles pushed up on his forehead. Then he disappeared into the shadows on land.

This was land I'd seen before and at night. I recognized the hill silhouetted against the sky. It was Placide Island. I couldn't see well enough to recognize which side of the island we were on, but I was willing to bet that it was just about the spot where the two men had been killed.

I'd seen enough. I took my gun from the bag around my neck and stepped out on the deck. I crouched down next to the cabin and waited for him to come clambering back over the prow.

Time passed slowly, but it passed and I finally realized that he should have been back before this. I stood up, peering toward the island. The light was worse, for it was near morning and the moon had just about finished its vigil, but I could see no sign of him. I took a couple of steps closer to the prow, staring at what I could see of the shoreline.

Something cold and sharp pressed against the side of my neck and slid quickly around to the front.

"Drop the gun, March," West Carroll said quietly from behind me.

TWELVE

We stood there, in a frozen tableau, for two or three minutes, although it seemed much longer. I could feel the sharp edge of the knife against my throat and knew that it would take only the slightest pressure to send it slicing through the skin. There was only one thing to do at the moment. I dropped the gun. It clattered on the deck.

"Move your foot very slowly," he said, "and push the gun back here."

I stretched out my foot until the heel hooked over the gun, then I pushed it as far back as I could. The pressure of the knife eased up slightly.

"Take a couple of slow steps forward," he said.

I obeyed. Then the knife left my throat and I knew that he had stooped and picked up the gun.

"Go sit on the deck right on the prow," he said. "You can turn around when you get there."

I walked to the prow and sat down. Then I swiveled to face him. He stood there, water dripping from him, holding my gun steadily. The knife was stuck through a loop on his trunks.

"Surprised, Mr. March?" he asked with a grin.

"Yeah," I admitted. Now I knew what had happened. He'd entered the water from another point and swum under the surface until he reached the rear of the boat. Then he had surfaced and climbed aboard. But what had made him do it? I had been very careful. What could have made him suspicious?

"I knew you were after me," he said arrogantly, "and I figured you'd probably try hiding on the boat. And I figured you wouldn't try anything until you'd seen everything you could. Did you see a lot, Mr. March?"

"Enough," I said. "But I'd guessed all of it before I saw it."

"You know what I carried ashore?"

"Heroin."

"Ten pounds of it this trip," he said. "You know how much that's worth?"

"More than both of us could spend easily," I said.

"Yeah, you're smart, Mr. March," he said. "You're smart if you figured out what was going on. Nobody else has. The only trouble is that you're not smart enough. Are you, Mr. March?"

"Not this time," I admitted. There was no point in arguing with him. He had the gun.

"I know your kind. You think you're so goddam smart that you can do everything yourself and that nobody can figure things out as well as you can. Maybe you'd have caught me if you'd told the Feds what you thought I was going to do. I don't think so, but maybe. Maybe you'd have gotten me all by yourself if you'd been satisfied to pull your gun on me when I picked up the heroin instead of waiting to see if I stashed it where you thought I would. Again, I don't think so, but maybe. But you had to prove how smart you are."

I had to admit that he was partly right.

"You know what you're going to get for your smartness?" he asked.

"The same thing the two men got," I said. "What did they do? Stumbled onto a rope tied to a tree and the other end going down into quicksand and got curious about what was at the other end of the rope?"

"Yeah. Only they didn't stumble. They had to be nosey. The rope was covered with branches so that no one could have seen it unless they were hunting around. But that ain't what's going to happen to you."

"Okay," I said wearily. "If you want to play games—what's going to happen to me?"

"I'm going to finish what I started day before yesterday. Then if they do find you, it'll still be an accident."

"I thought it wasn't any accident the other day," I said.

"Of course it wasn't. It would have worked, too, if that damn boat had stayed away. As soon as I saw it hit you, I surfaced to be sure everything was clear, and there was that damn boat no more than twenty feet away. So I had to go down and save you. But it won't happen this time."

"Don't you see," I asked, "that nobody is going to believe I could have the same accident twice with you?"

"Who said with me? I won't have been anywhere near the scene. And anything can happen with an inexperienced diver."

"Who did I go out with?"

"How the hell do I know? Let the cops find out. Plenty of witnesses saw me when I left the dock and they'll swear I was alone. And that's the way it's going to be—unless you try something while we're getting there. In that case I'll have to spoil it by putting a bullet through you."

He started the motor and backed away from shore, then swung the boat in a wide circle heading back the way we had come. He was steering with one hand, holding the gun with the other.

I didn't have a chance to try anything while he was holding the gun. He was all of six feet from me and I was sitting down. I'd have a better chance even with an empty oxygen tank.

Daylight came just as we entered the Gulf. The early grayness was gone and the sun was just beginning to peep over the horizon when we reached a spot that looked as if it was near where we had been two days before. He slowly brought the boat to a stop. He backed into the cabin, still holding the gun on me, and felt around until he found an oxygen tank, goggles, and flippers. He tossed them over to me.

"Put them on," he said.

I put on the flippers and the goggles and strapped the oxygen tank to my back. I left the mouthpiece hanging down on my chest.

"All right, March," he said. "You've had it. Over the side."

As I adjusted the mouthpiece, I was thinking that there might be enough oxygen in the tank to let me swim under water far enough to get out of range of the gun. Of course, he'd come after me with the boat, but I might have a chance to get away. Slim, but still a chance. Then he knocked that idea in the head.

"I'm going over with you," he said. His free hand stroked the long-bladed knife at his waist. "Just to make sure you don't get away."

The mouthpiece was fitting all right. I stood up and dived over the side. I surfaced almost immediately, lifting the goggles so I could breathe through my nose and save as much oxygen as possible. I was just in time to see his feet vanishing beneath the water. I watched, hoping he'd come up near me and I could slug him before he got his bearings. But he was too smart for that. He surfaced about fifteen feet from me. He dropped his mouthpiece and raised the hand holding the knife.

"Go down," he said, "and stay down, if you don't want me to use this."

This was as bad as the gun. He was a better swimmer than I was, and that knife was a wicked weapon. I pulled my goggles down and dived. I only went about ten feet below the surface; the farther down I went, the quicker the oxygen would go.

He appeared several feet to my right. Still too far away. If I could only get him where there was a chance of grabbing the knife. He was motioning me to go farther down. Then I had an idea.

I turned and swam down, hoping he wasn't too certain exactly how much oxygen there was in the tank. I didn't dare wait too long. Once the oxygen was gone, it would be too late to do anything. In the meantime I breathed as sparingly as I could.

When I was down about forty feet I decided to try it. I tried to remember how I had reacted two days before. I was sure that Carroll must have emptied the reserve tank. I reached around and turned it on. I waited a second, then pushed myself upward in frantic haste. I got a glimpse of Carroll about fifteen feet above me. I tried to do everything I remembered from two days before. I struggled more and more frantically, then went limp and let myself drift upward, my head down. I was barely breathing at first, then I held my breath, for I knew the bubbles from the exhale tube would be a giveaway. I kept my eyes open just enough so that I could see.

He approached carefully, stopping several times to stare at me. I knew I couldn't hold my breath much longer. Finally he pushed himself in close and started to reach for me with his free hand.

There was no point in trying to hit him under water; it would be impossible to get enough power into it to hurt him. I took a deep breath and grabbed for the hand that held the knife. I got my fingers on his wrist before he reacted by exploding into action. At first he tried to twist away, but I tightened my grip and he didn't succeed. Then he turned and began clawing at my mouthpiece with his free hand. I ignored that and concentrated on just getting the knife away from him. I got both hands on him, one on his wrist and the other on his hand. I began to twist. Suddenly I felt the knife loosen in his hand. I doubled the pressure and then the knife slipped from his hand. I almost missed it, but got it just before it sank.

He was still tearing at my mouthpiece. I brought the knife up quickly and cut the two tubes that led from his mouthpiece. His face twisted in sudden consternation. I knocked his other hand away and shot toward the surface even as he started his first kick.

As I came out of the water, I looked around for the boat. I was about ten feet from it. I threw the knife and it clattered on the deck. I turned my attention to the water just in time to see his head emerging. I grabbed him by the hair with my left hand, pulling him up faster. As his jaw came into sight, I hit as hard as I could. His head snapped back and I knew he was out. I threw my arm around his neck and swam with him to the boat.

It was quite a job dragging him onto the boat, but I finally made it. By the time I did, however, all I wanted to do was rest, but I knew he wouldn't stay unconscious long. I dragged him into the cabin and started looking for something to tie him with. I found a thin rope in a cabinet. There was something else there, too, but I didn't look closer for the moment. I used the rope to truss him up. When I was sure the knots were tight enough to keep him, I went back to the cabinet.

What I'd seen was a map. An old one. Somebody had penciled "Placide Island" on it.

When I turned back, Carroll's eyes were open. "That," I said, indicating the map, "might be just the little extra gimmick to hang you, my friend."

He called me a colorful name, but one that was hardly admissible in polite society. I grinned at him and went out. I'd never operated a boat like this, but a little fooling around showed me the rudiments. I got it started and headed in the general direction of New Orleans.

A number of the boats were going out with fishing parties as I neared the docks. I managed successfully to avoid running into any of them. I was proud of myself. Several boatmen looked at me curiously as they passed. They probably recognized the boat and wondered what I was doing on it.

Throwing the engine into reverse was a little too delicate for me. I misjudged it the first time and bounced off the dock, leaving a considerable dent in the wood. The second time I made it with only a little bump. I cut the motor and tossed the mooring rope over its post. There were only a couple of people on the pier, down at the far end, but I didn't want to take any chance. I went into the cabin and searched through the storage space. I found a sheet and tore a strip from it. I used it to gag Carroll. He tried to bite me when I forced it into his mouth. I looked in his pocket and found a dime.

"Relax, buster," I told him. "Soon, you can talk your head off if you want to."

I went out and jumped off the boat. There was a coffee shop across the street from the pier and I headed for it. They did have a public phone in it—very public, because there wasn't a booth. I looked at the clock. It was just six in the morning. I put the coin in the phone and dialed Lieutenant Stern's home number. He answered on the second ring.

"This is Milo," I said. "Were you about ready to leave?"

"Soon as I finish my coffee," he said.

"Stop off and see me on your way to the office," I said. "Only don't keep me waiting too long."

"What's up?" he asked quickly.

"Everything," I said.

"You can't talk?"

"No."

"Where are you?"

"The pier."

"I'll be right there," he said and hung up. I left the restaurant and walked quickly back to the boat. Nobody had approached it. I jumped on the deck and looked inside the cabin. Carroll was still as I had left him. I went back on deck and waited.

It was about twenty minutes later when Stern arrived. He parked out at the edge of the pier. He climbed out and looked around. I stood up on the deck and waved when he looked in my direction. He started walking over.

"Been swimming a little early, haven't you?" he asked when he arrived in front of the boat.

"Early or late," I said. "Depends on how you look at it. Come aboard."

He jumped up on the deck. I saw his gaze flick over the boat and hesitate when it came to the cabin. "Friend of yours?" he asked mildly.

"The murderer," I said. "West Carroll."

He glanced at me briefly. "He confessed to you?"

"No. Come in and I'll show you the two tangible clues. Then I'll tell you the rest of it." He followed me into the cabin. I opened the door of the cabinet. "There's the missing map of Placide Island, which was taken from the body of one of the men. And there"—I kicked the knife that was on the floor—"is one of his knives. He's got another around someplace. You can match one of them up with the wounds. That and opportunity and motive ought to be enough."

"What made you get on to him?" Stern asked curiously.

"The Purloined Letter."

"What letter?"

"A story by Edgar Allan Poe," I said with a grin. "They're searching all over for the stolen letter and all the time it's lying out in plain sight. I knew something bothered me about Carroll, but it didn't begin to fall into place until he tried to kill me two days ago. We kept trying to figure out how Lane could get away from two witnesses to kill the men or how the killer could have reached the island without Carroll hearing him, and overlooked the fact that nobody was watching Carroll. All he had to do was climb off the boat, follow them and kill them, and go back and wait."

"And the motive?"

"Look," I said, "it's a long story. I've got some clothes in my car here. Let me get dressed and I'll tell it to you at headquarters."

"All right," he said. "Let's untie him and I'll take him in."

"Want me to leave my car here and help you?" I asked as we started to loosen the knots.

"I can take him," he said.

We got the ropes off Carroll and the gag out of his mouth. Stern put handcuffs on him and led him away. I hurried down to my car, put on my clothes, and headed downtown. Stern was waiting in his office when I got there.

"The lab is working on the map and knives now," he said. "They say there are a lot of fingerprints on the map and they may be able to match the knife to the wounds. But it still won't be a lot."

"Opportunity and motive," I said. "Besides, there will be others in the net. You might get one of them to talk."

"I'm waiting for you to talk first."

"Okay. Remember we were talking about drug smuggling the other day?"

He nodded.

"It's been operating on a big scale through here for years. Both the FBI and the Treasury Department have been working on it and getting nowhere. It's a Syndicate operation and the man in charge of this section is Raoul Rouen. The Federal men know it and I know it, but so far there's no proof. They also have a list of other suspects they've been watching, including our friend the undertaker, Adam Perrin. But they've never been able to discover the slightest connection between any of their suspects."

"And you've discovered it?"

"I have," I said firmly.

"Maybe we'd better call them in on this session."

"Later," I said. "As soon as I knew that Rouen's chief business was drugs and that he was anxious to not have the murder solved, I was sure the two men must have stumbled onto something about the drugs. But what? When I went out to look at the island, you remember I found the spot where the men were killed. It was at the edge of a quicksand pit. There was a small tree right there, too, and there were rope strands clinging to the bark—only I didn't think anything of it at the time."

"Hiding place for the narcotics?" he asked.

I nodded. "Another problem which had to be solved to get to the main problem was how the drugs were smuggled into New Orleans. It had to be something pretty clever to fool both the G-men and the T-men this long. They knew the drugs came out of Italy, and they've been checking every ship on each end. And they've been watching all their suspects, including Rouen. Eddie Capo visits Rouen regularly, but the old man claims he's interested in Eddie's reformation. The only other person to visit him regularly is Narcisse Coillon. But he's a poor relation of the old man, and the Federal men haven't suspected him. I did, mostly because, being a guide, he can get around to all sorts of places without anyone suspecting him much."

"He's in it, too?" Stern asked.

"Up to his neck. I had him followed the other night. He left Rouen's and went out on the river in his boat, heading in the direction of Placide Island. When he returned, he was carrying something large and bulky in a gunnysack. He went over back of Adam Perrin's funeral parlor and left it there. Maybe inside, maybe somewhere outside. The next day I had Perrin followed. So did you. It was quite a procession. Perrin certainly didn't take any bulky package out, but it would be easy to conceal several pounds of heroin on your person without its showing. Perrin wandered aimlessly around town, making fifteen different stops. I think one of those stops was a drop for the heroin, but I don't know which one or who picks it up from there. But you can be sure that whoever it is never meets Perrin face to face."

"If the package Coillon carried was so bulky," Stern asked, "how could Perrin conceal the same package without it showing?"

"Now," I said, "we come to the guessing part—only it worked out. I knew the Federal men had been trying for months to find out how the drugs were smuggled in. They know their business, so it meant the gang had to have something pretty clever. That, in turn, implied some sort of container which was the secret of their success. It seemed logical to me that the drugs were stashed in the container and that was why Coillon's package was so bulky. Perrin then removed the heroin and took it on the next leg of its journey. But what about the container? If the container was special enough to fool the Feds, then it might be something dangerous to just toss out with the garbage. And it would be dangerous for Perrin to keep it."

"Looks like Perrin is turning into a key man."

"I think he is. And in a way, he's like the purloined letter, too. That red hearse. Everybody took it for granted even when they suspected him. And Perrin had a perfect way of getting rid of anything. I don't know about the others, but this time the container was put into a coffin to keep the corpse company. Perrin had a funeral that same afternoon."

"How do you know this?" Stern asked.

"I went to Saint Roch cemetery night before last and looked in the coffin," I said. "It was there and still is."

He groaned. "I'll pretend I didn't hear the first part of that," he said. "And for God's sake, don't repeat it. Don't you know that's against the law?"

"Is it?" I asked innocently. I grinned at him. "Don't you want to know what the container was?"

"What?"

"Were you in the Second World War?"

He nodded.

"Well, you may remember that there were nasty little torpedo-like mines that were attached to the bottoms of ships so they would explode sometime after leaving the harbor. They were either magnetic or attached by clamps. Both sides kept frogmen busy attaching them or trying to find the ones that had been attached before they went off."

He nodded again.

"That was the container. One of those mines with the mechanism removed. You take the head off and there's a nice hollow space to put heroin in. A diver went down in the Italian harbor at night and attached the mine, and then another diver met the ship out in the Gulf here and removed it. They probably picked only ships that would reach here at night."

"Clever," he said. "Carroll was the man here?"

"Yeah. I thought he was the pickup man even before. I checked back. On the night that the three men were on Placide Island, Carroll came back to the dock at a time to coincide with a time schedule for having met a ship that arrived that night."

"If the members of the gang were so careful not to be seen together, how come Coillon hired Carroll that night?"

"He didn't. He'd hired another boatman, but that one never showed up. It was one of the three treasure seekers who hired Carroll, and Coillon tried to dissuade him. Normally, I imagine, Carroll would have refused to take them. But he knew that he'd just left a batch of heroin on Placide Island and he probably agreed so that he could keep a watch on them. When the two men, Bryant and Mack, left the others and headed in the direction of the hiding place, Coillon warned Carroll."

"How?"

"Look at Lane's testimony again. He made a big deal about Coillon trying to stop the two men from going off alone, even going so far as to shout after them when they had already started. That warned Carroll. He followed them."

"Where were the drugs hidden?"

"A rope was tied to the container and to the tree. Then the container was let down into the quicksand and the rope covered with branches and leaves. The two men must have accidentally uncovered the rope and were curious about what was on the other end. If they hadn't discovered it, I imagine he wouldn't have killed them."

"And the bodies?"

"I don't know, but I think Carroll must have dragged them back to the boat and hidden them. Then Perrin got them early the next morning and they worked up the story about the empty house. Or maybe Carroll put the bodies in the empty house during the night and Perrin did pick them up there."

"Probably they worked it that way," he said.

"But to get back to Carroll," I said, "the night he took me to Placide, he made it clear that he had to be back at the dock by ten-thirty. And when we got back, he headed out toward the Gulf. There was an Italian freighter arriving that night. And that was the load of heroin Coillon picked up three nights ago. The next Italian ship was one docking at five o'clock this morning. So last night I went down and hid on Carroll's boat. I saw him dive and come up with the mine from the freighter. And I saw him take it ashore on Placide."

"Smart work," Stern said.

"Not smart enough," I said. "I didn't really start thinking

about Carroll until he tried to kill me. And last night I was careless enough to let him get the drop on me. I was lucky he didn't succeed the second time."

"Yeah," he said thoughtfully. "You say there's a cache of drugs there on the island now?"

"Yes."

"We'd better have it picked up," he said, reaching for the phone.

"No," I said sharply. He stopped and looked at me. "You pick it up and you'll never get anything on the others. Leave it there and you can. Now, all of this is pertinent to your case, so you ought to be in on it. But maybe you'd better call the FBI and Treasury and let them sit in with you."

"I intended to," he said. "As a matter of fact, I'll call our Narcotics Squad, too. You got anything else for me?"

"No."

"You ready to talk to them?"

"Sure."

"You can make your suggestion about how to handle the rest of it," he said, "but from here on I'll have to take a back seat, too, so they may pay no attention to you." He picked up the phone and made his calls.

A half hour later there were five of us in Stern's office. A lieutenant from the New Orleans Narcotics Squad and the two Federal men, in addition to Stern and me. One of the Federal men was the one I had talked to in his office.

"What happened with you last night?" he asked me coldly as he came in.

"I went out the back way," I said with a grin.

"Okay," he said grimly. "Let's hear your story."

I repeated everything I had told Stern. "Now," I concluded, "if you pick up this last shipment, you won't get anything on the others. Even if you find the other container in the coffin where I think it is"—I stopped and smiled innocently at Stern—"you won't have enough on Perrin. So I have a suggestion."

"What?" one of the Federal men asked.

"Coillon will probably pick up the stuff tonight or tomorrow night. Don't put a tail on him. We can wait down by the docks—and I do mean *we* because you're not crowding me out of the finish—and follow him when he drops it for Perrin. Then we follow Perrin and this time get the next step. Then you can net all of them."

The two Federal men exchanged glances. "We intend something of the sort," he said, "but we can hardly take just anybody along on the job."

"Look, buster," I said, "I've done more of this kind of work than you have. Try to cut me out and I'll blow the gaff on the whole thing."

"Well ... ," he said. "What do you think, Lieutenant?" he asked the man from the Narcotics Squad.

"Well, he has done most of the work so far," the Lieutenant said. "And he's succeeded where the rest of us failed. So maybe we can use him."

"All right," the Federal man said, but he wasn't happy about it. "We'll put a man on the docks just in case they move before we expect it. Then we'll take over tonight. You working with us, Lieutenant?"

He nodded.

"Lieutenant Stern?"

"I'd like to," Stern said. "It is tied in with the motive on my murder case."

"All right, the five of us will cover it. We'll use one of our cars and meet here at, say, six o'clock."

"Why not use my car?" I suggested. "Then, if they do spot it, they'll think it's just me messing into the case and not the regular cops."

"Might be a good idea," the second Federal man said.

"All right," the first one said, nodding. "Here at six o'clock tonight." He stood up.

"While you're at it," I said, "you might as well pull that tail off me. He hasn't had much success anyway." The Federal man glared at me. Lieutenant Stern hid a grin behind his hand.

"Don't feel bad about it," I told the Federal man. I stood up, realizing how tired I was. "You were a big help to me and I'm sure you will be again tonight." I winked at Stern and walked out while I was ahead.

THIRTEEN

Back at the hotel I called Lisette and told her I was sorry but I couldn't see her that night because I had to work. She jumped to the conclusion that I had failed the night before. I didn't correct her because I couldn't be sure that the operator wasn't listening in. She sounded worried about me, but I assured her that I'd be all right and that I'd call her the first chance I got. Then I hung up and went to sleep.

I was awakened once when Willie called. I told him there wasn't anything for him to do, but he was still on the payroll.

"That isn't the only reason I called," he said. "I decided to go up and watch the Rouen house for a while last night, even though you said I didn't have to. About twelve-thirty, or a little after, that fellow—what's his name, Capo?"

"Yeah."

"Well, he came dashing out of the house, jumped into his car, and roared away.

There wasn't any chance to follow him. Then he came back about forty minutes later."

"Probably remembered he hadn't killed anyone all day," I said sleepily, "and went out to fix it. I'll talk to you tomorrow, Willie." I was back asleep by the time the receiver was back on the phone.

It was late afternoon when I awakened. I just had time to

grab something to eat and get down to Lieutenant Stern's office. The other men were already there. The five of us got into my car and drove down to the pier. I parked where they told me to and we settled back to wait.

It was a long vigil. Three times one of us went to the restaurant and brought back coffee in containers. And waited some more. But it was useless. There was no sign of Narcisse Coillon throughout the long night. Shortly after dawn, two other Federal men showed up and we left. I drove them back to police headquarters.

"Tonight at the same time," the Federal man said. I nodded and drove away.

Again I called Lisette and went to bed. Before I went to sleep, I told the operator not to bother me.

That afternoon I was up in time to shower leisurely and shave and then call Lisette again before I went downstairs. I assured her that this would soon be over and we could have fun again. I promised I'd be careful and hung up.

At six o'clock I was once more at police headquarters. The five of us got into the Cadillac and went to the pier, parking in the same spot we had the night before. We settled down to the long wait.

It was about one o'clock in the morning and we had gone once for containers of coffee, when the quiet of the night was shattered by a short whine of a police siren three or four blocks north of us. It whined twice more, then was silent.

"Well," Lieutenant Stern said, "Coillon's coming."

"How do you know?" I asked.

"One of our patrol cars has been covering the area," he said.

"When they spotted him, they were to go north several blocks and then give three blasts on the siren. That was it."

The Federal man who was sitting next to me leaned partly out the window and I saw he was holding something in his hands. "What's that?" I asked.

"Camera," he said, "with infrared film."

A few minutes later Narcisse Coillon came into sight a couple of blocks away. He was walking and it was obvious that he was being careful to make sure he wasn't being followed. He was probably nervous. Nothing had yet been given to the papers about the arrest of West Carroll, but somebody in the gang probably knew he was missing, and that would be enough for them all to get a little nervous.

When he reached the pier, Coillon stopped and stood for several minutes, using the pretense of lighting a cigarette. When he was sure there was no one around, he went on and got into his boat. He cast off and started the motor. The little boat moved away slowly, heading in the direction of Placide Island.

As soon as it was out of sight, one of the Federal men jumped out of the car and went into the restaurant. He was back in about five minutes.

"Okay," he said as he got in.

"Okay what?" I asked.

"We're sending a small plane over the island. He'll time it so he can get pictures of Coillon as he picks up the drugs."

"Smart," I said.

He grunted as if to say he didn't care whether I thought he was smart or not. I grinned to myself in the dark.

Once again we waited, this time without smoking because Coillon approaching from the water might see the glow of our cigarettes long before we could see him. It was well over an hour before we heard the putt-putt of his motor, and a few minutes later his boat nosed into the dock. When he got out he had a gunnysack slung over his shoulder. Knowing what it was, I could make out the outlines of the torpedo shape. He walked up the street, stopping every few feet to check. The Federal man next to me was busy taking pictures. Coillon vanished into the shadows when he was two blocks away.

"Now?" I asked.

"Wait," the Federal man said.

The only traffic was several blocks away, so it was quiet on the pier. We waited and listened, and a few minutes later we heard a car start up. It sounded as if it were about four blocks away.

"Okay," the Federal man said. "Get going. Take the shortest route to the funeral parlor. We want to get there before he does."

I started the motor and drove the Cadillac around the corner before turning on the lights. "Maybe we should follow him," I said. "Perrin might not be the only drop."

"He'll be followed. We've got men on every single street leading away from this section. They all have a description of Coillon's car and the license number. Whoever follows him will drop out as soon as Coillon reaches Perrin's."

One thing I had to admit. Once they started rolling, they were thorough. "With pictures?" I asked.

"Yes. He'll be photographed every foot of the way." By this

time I knew the route from the pier to Perdido Street pretty well and I pushed the Cadillac as fast as it was safe. When we got there, I turned into the side street that ran past one end of the alley.

"Drive up past it and turn around and come back," the Federal man said. I did as he told me. "This the spot where he entered the alley?" he asked.

"I think so," I said. "That's the way it was told to me."

"All right. Go around to the other end of the alley and park near it."

I drove around the block. As I turned down the side street, I switched off my lights and the motor and coasted to a parking place next to the mouth of the alley. The man beside me grunted again, but this time he sounded as if he was pleased with me.

From where we sat we could see partway into the alley, far enough to detect any light that flashed into it. About ten minutes after we parked, we heard the car on the other block and then we saw the headlights briefly as he turned into the alley before they flicked out. The man next to me was out of the car swiftly and silently. He knelt at the edge of the alley, shoved his camera forward, and began taking pictures.

A few minutes later he got back into the car. He held the door without closing it. "Get out of here," he said, "before he drives out of the alley. He's starting now."

I had the car under way before he finished speaking. I didn't turn on the lights until we were around the corner on Perdido Street.

"Double back on the next block," he said. "When you hit

the next street, there's a stop sign. Wait there until I tell you to go on."

I took a left turn at the next street and drove another block. There was a stop sign there. I stopped and waited, but not for long. It was maybe only a minute when a car came by. It was Coillon. Then about a hundred yards behind him came another car, a beat-up old Ford.

"All right," the Federal man said. "It looks as if he's on his way home. And we've got him covered. Let's go."

"Where?"

"Back to police headquarters."

"That's all?" I asked.

"If you're right," he said grimly, "that's all for tonight. In the meantime we've got a man at either end of that alley and another one in front of the funeral parlor. So if you're wrong, we'll still have it covered."

"You're using a lot of men," I said.

"We pulled in our men from Baton Rouge and Shreveport," he said.

"When you were at the edge of the alley," I said, "could you see if he put the sack in the funeral parlor, or met Perrin and handed it to him?"

He hesitated, but only for a minute. "He did neither," he said. "There's some sort of building at the rear of the funeral parlor. It may be a storage building or something of the sort. He put the sack and its contents in there. The photographs may show more than I could see."

We arrived at police headquarters and the four men got out. "Tomorrow morning at eight," the Federal man said.

"I'll be here," I told him. I drove straight back to the hotel. It was four in the morning. I left a call for seven and tumbled into bed.

It seemed to me I had barely gotten into bed when the phone rang and the operator was telling me to get up. I thanked her and pushed myself out of bed. A fast shower helped a little, but not too much. So I had a drink before I went down for my coffee.

It was just eight o'clock when I picked up the four men. We drove straight to Perdido Street and parked about a block from the funeral parlor. A few minutes after we parked, an old car pulled out from across the street and left. It was the other Federal man going home.

"What about the two men on the alley?" I asked.

"They'll stay there until we're sure," he said.

"Where's your man?" I asked Lieutenant Stern.

"I pulled him off," he said, "as soon as this operation started."

It was another long wait. Sometimes that's what good police work means: the patience to just wait. It was almost noon when Adam Perrin came out of the funeral parlor and got into the red hearse. He wasn't carrying anything, but no one would ever call him a natty dresser and he could have been carrying quite a bit of heroin on him without its showing.

"Think you can follow him all right?" the Federal man asked.

I didn't bother to answer him. When the red hearse pulled away from the curb, I followed, letting another car get in between the hearse and my car.

"Perrin live there, too?" I asked.

"Upstairs," the Federal man said.

"Family?"

"No. He lives alone."

"Your boys going in to look it over now that he's out?" I asked.

He glanced at me. "That would be breaking and entering," he said. But from the way he said it, I knew they were.

"Heaven forfend," I said and concentrated on my driving.

Adam Perrin took us on the same sort of merry chase that he had Willie and the city cop a few days earlier. In the next three hours he made twelve stops in various parts of New Orleans. Ten of the stops were at apartment houses. I noticed the Federal man was writing down the addresses.

After the twelfth stop, Perrin drove straight back to his funeral parlor and went inside. We drove a half block past it and parked.

"Wait," the Federal man said. He opened the door and got out. He walked up the street and went into a candy and tobacco store. Another man entered right on his heels, and I was sure it was another agent.

He came back in ten minutes and slid into the seat beside me.

"Did they find anything?" I asked. He glanced at me and I grinned. Finally, he grinned back.

"They found the mine that was used as the container," he said, "but nothing else. So he must have dropped the heroin somewhere. The question is where."

"Let me see the list you made," I said.

He dug it out and spread it on his knee so I could see it. I got out the list that Willie had given me and held it beside his.

"These are the stops he made the other day," I said. "It helps a little, but not much. There are eight addresses that are on both lists. You said that you've had a number of suspects?"

He nodded.

"Well, you can check those eight addresses and see if any of your suspects live at them. If that doesn't work, you can always start checking all the apartments. Send a man around asking to borrow a cup of heroin."

He wasn't amused. "A hundred and twenty apartments," he said. "In the meantime, if you're right, we've lost ten pounds of heroin."

"What do we do now?" I asked.

"You drive us back to police headquarters," he said. "Then we go to work trying to run down that heroin before they get it out of the city. We'll keep men on Perrin and Coillon and Rouen instead of picking them up yet. Lieutenant, I think we'll take another crack at Carroll and see if we can get anything out of him."

"Okay," Lieutenant Stern said.

"Nobody asked me," I said, starting the car, "but you can bet there is one place that heroin won't be. Rouen's. And so you won't have anything on him."

"Probably not," the Federal man admitted. "Unless somebody talks. But we hadn't really expected to get him. If, however, we can ruin his organization, we'll settle for that."

"Too bad," I said.

"What can you do?" he asked. "The big ones like him

seldom go near the stuff, so it's hard to pin it on them. When we get them, we usually get them on something else."

"Yeah," I said. "Now, what do I do in this operation?"

"Go back to New York," he said. "There's nothing you can do now except get in the way. Besides, your own case is finished."

"Swept aside like a discarded mistress," I said with mock bitterness.

"Don't misunderstand us, March. We're very grateful for what you've done, but there isn't anything else you can do."

"If you do go right back to New York," Lieutenant Stern said, "don't forget that we'll need your testimony when Carroll goes on trial."

"I'll come back," I said. "Just let me know."

I let the men out at police headquarters. The Federal men were in such a hurry they hardly said good-bye. I told Stern I'd talk to him before I left. I drove back to the hotel.

I stopped in at the bar for a drink. I'd been so busy the past two days I'd gotten behind on my drinking. While I was having the first one, a call came for me. It was Willie. He was only a few blocks away, so I told him to meet me outside the hotel. I finished my drink and went out.

"It looks like it's all over, Willie," I told him when we met. "You and I are both out of it, so here's your money. And thanks."

"Got it all solved?" he asked.

"Only partly," I said. "But the place is knee-deep in cops and they don't want any competition. Anyway, you and I got the murderer and three of the drug ring."

"Coillon and Perrin?"

"And Carroll, who is also the murderer," I said. "And you, Willie, were half the battle."

"Thanks for the chance," he said. "You going back to New York?"

"Probably," I said. "Are you going back to that divining jazz?"

"It's almost time for me to go back to school," he said, "so I may use the rest of the time for my vacation."

"Okay," I said. "Thanks, again, Willie. And good luck." I shook hands with him and went back to the hotel. I went into a phone booth and called Lisette. She answered after the fourth ring, sounding out of breath.

"Where were you running from?" I asked.

"Oh, I had started out," she said. "I was in the hall and had to unlock the door again. I'm in a hurry anyway, so I guess I was rushing. How are you, darling?"

"All right, I guess," I said. "It looks like it might be all wrapped up, so I'll be over to pick you up tonight."

"Really?" she said. "That's wonderful, darling. But I'll have to hurry twice as fast if I have to make myself pretty for you. I've got to run now. I'll see you tonight."

"Okay," I said. I hung up and went back to the bar. I had two more drinks and then I went upstairs. I unlocked the door and went in. Then I stopped. Eddie Capo stood in the center of the room, a gun in his hand.

FOURTEEN

Once again I was taken by surprise. I hadn't been expecting Eddie. I guess in the excitement of the past two days I'd even forgotten that Eddie was waiting to be unleashed.

"Just take it easy, sucker," Eddie said. "Don't reach for anything and don't make no sudden moves. If I have to do it here, I will."

"Go home, Eddie," I said. "I don't feel like listening to your threats today."

"You've been a busy guy," Eddie said. "We just found out today about West Carroll. In the can charged with murder. And you brought him in. Real cute, too. It's kept hushed up, so maybe we don't know anything's happening. Well, sucker, this time there's no threats. The boss said yes, just like I knew he would. He knows that I was right and maybe it's too late, but it'll make the next sucker think twice before he tries to move in."

"You'll never make it, Eddie," I said.

"Guess again," he said. His eyes were bright and feverish. "I'm going to waltz you right out of here like you were a tame bear, and you won't be coming back. Take your coat off and let it fall to the floor. But move real slow."

I slipped my arms out of my coat and let it drop, watching Eddie closely. There was no doubt that he was ready to kill. If

I was going to make a break, it would almost have to be before we got away from the hotel.

"Now reach up and unbuckle the shoulder holster and let it drop," he said. "Slow—or the road will end right here."

I reached up and fumbled with the buckle. I was beginning to feel that it was now or never. The tension was building up in me. I could feel it like a hard ball in the pit of my stomach. I let my hands drop partway without unfastening the shoulder harness.

"No," I said. "You want my gun, you come and take it."

For a minute I thought he was just going to shoot. But he had enough intelligence to know that the hotel room was not a good place.

"Okay," he said. "Turn around with your back to me and lift your hands over your head."

I started to turn and lift my hands at the same time. Then, when I was half turned, I dived headlong for the bed, grabbing my gun out of the holster as I went.

The shot sounded like a cannon in the small room. Something plucked at my left shoulder. Then I was on the bed, rolling to free my right arm. He shot again and I heard plaster fall behind me. I ignored his gun, which was lining up on me again. I raised my gun slowly and squeezed the trigger. It bucked in my hand and Eddie spun half around, his shirt blooming red over the right shoulder. The gun dropped from his hand.

He turned back, his face tight with pain. He looked at me for a second, then started to bend over to pick up the gun with his left hand. I aimed carefully and put a bullet through his left hand.

I could hear the breath hiss through his teeth, but that was the only sound he made. He straightened up and stood staring at me, blood dripping to the floor from his shoulder and hand. I got up off the bed and walked over to where his gun had fallen. Eddie kicked at me, but I avoided it easily. I used my foot to shove the gun farther away from him. Then I bent and picked it up with my left hand. As I straightened up, there was a twinge of pain in my left shoulder. I looked down and was surprised to see my shoulder was all red, too. I thought he had missed me completely.

Keeping my gaze on him, I unbuttoned my shirt and spread it so I could take a quick look at my shoulder. There was a furrow across the top of it, the blood welling up from it. It was going to be painful for a few days, but that would be all.

The phone rang. I backed up to it, picked up the receiver. "Yeah?" I said.

"This is the desk clerk," a voice said. "Somebody just phoned down and said they heard several shots in your room."

"I'm afraid they have too much imagination," I said. "I just knocked over a chair."

"Sorry," he said.

I depressed the bar on the phone and waited a couple of seconds. Then I let it up. When the operator answered, I gave her Lieutenant Stern's number.

"Milo," I said when he came on. "I've got a customer up here in my hotel room for you. Better get up here fast before he bleeds to death."

"Be right there," he said and hung up.

I pushed the bar down again and waited. Then I let it up and told the operator to give me the bell captain. "You got a boy named Jack working for you?" I asked.

"Yes," he said. "Who is this?"

"Mr. March in three seventeen. Is he on duty now?"

"Yes, sir."

"Let me talk to him."

I waited and after a couple of minutes a different voice said hello.

"Jack?" I asked.

"Yes, sir."

"This is the man who had a phobia and went out through the kitchen door the other night. Remember me?"

"Yes, sir."

"Okay. I'm in three seventeen. Run into the drugstore and get some gauze and adhesive tape and bring it up here. And hurry because we don't have too much time." I hung up and took a good look at Eddie. He was still standing there, but he looked paler. "You'd better sit down," I told him, "before you faint on me."

"I've been shot before," he said between clenched teeth. But he moved over and sat in the chair.

"Sure you have," I said, "and will be again. You're a big brave man. But you might still faint. And as far as I'm concerned, you can bleed to death. I didn't shoot to kill, but that's the most I'll do for you."

He called me a dirty name, which I ignored.

A few minutes later there was a knock on the door. "Come in," I yelled. The door opened and the bellhop stepped inside. He took in the picture in one glance, but didn't say anything. He just closed the door fast and waited for me to tell him what I wanted done.

"There'll be a cop here soon to collect that one," I said. "I don't want him to know I got hit, too. He might want to take me to a doctor, and I have things to do. Come over and fix me up."

He came over and put the gauze and tape on the bed. "What shall I do, sir?" he asked.

"Pull my shirt back off the shoulder," I said. He obeyed. "Now pick up that bottle of whiskey and splash some over it. We don't have anything else, so we'll have to use that. If it doesn't do anything else, it'll make the germs too drunk to do anything."

"You ought to see a doctor, sir," he said. But he was getting the whiskey while he talked.

"Later," I said.

He poured whiskey on the wound and I gritted my teeth. It hurt like hell.

"Now," I said, "wad up some of that gauze and put it over the wound and tape it there."

He did as I'd told him, moving swiftly, and it was soon done. It should be all right for a couple of hours. I pulled my shirt into place and buttoned it. I thought to hell with the tie and pulled it off.

"Help me into my coat," I told him.

He picked up the coat and helped me work my left arm into it. The shoulder was already beginning to stiffen. I switched the gun to my left hand and dug ten dollars out of my pocket.

"Better get out fast," I said. "Take the gauze and tape with you. And keep quiet."

He nodded and left quickly. I looked down at myself. If I kept the coat buttoned, none of the blood would show. I reached down for the bottle of whiskey and took a big drink from it.

There was another knock on the door and I yelled for him to come in. The door opened and it was Lieutenant Stern. He looked around the room and whistled.

"What happened?" he asked.

"Eddie was here when I came in," I said. "He tried to gun me, but missed with both shots. You'll be able to dig the bullets out of the wall later. I had to stop him. I had better luck."

He looked at Eddie. "Why twice?"

"I got him in the shoulder first and he dropped the gun. Then he tried to pick it up with his left hand. I could have killed him, but I thought I'd save him for you."

"You charging him?"

"Yeah," I said. "Breaking and entering, assault with a deadly weapon, and attempted murder. And anything else you can think up. You better get him out of here before he bleeds to death."

Stern nodded. "I'll send the boys up to go over the room."

"Okay," I said.

Stern picked up Eddie's gun and slipped it in his pocket. He went over to Eddie. "Come on," he said.

Eddie got up, swaying a little, but he stayed upright. He walked out of the room ahead of Stern.

I sat down on the edge of the bed. I picked up the bottle and took another drink. Finding Eddie in my room had jarred me into thinking about my first brush with him—and about a lot of things that had happened since then.

I picked up the phone and called the Federal man. He was in.

"March," I said. "Remember the day you told me that the New York police had just grabbed a member of the gang that was trying to hijack Rouen's outfit and he was talking?"

"Yes."

"Was his name Lew Manton?" I asked.

"Yes," he said. "Why?"

"Just wanted to check and see if my crystal ball was still working," I told him and hung up.

I thought some more, trying to sort out the things I had to do and the time in which I had to do them. I picked up the phone and called the airport. I asked about the next flight to New York. It was an hour off.

I went down and got in the Cadillac. I drove until I reached the big white house. I drove around to the back and parked. I went over and tried the back door. It was unlocked. I opened it and walked in. Just as I reached the stairs, I passed a startled-looking servant, but I paid no attention to him. I went on up to the second floor and down to the study. I kicked the door open.

Rouen was sitting behind the desk. He looked up as the door swung open and his face paled as he saw me. Then he tried to smile. It was only partly successful.

"Well, Mr. March," he said. "I was just thinking about you."

"Sure you were," I said. "You were wondering if Eddie Capo had killed me yet."

He made a gesture with his hand as though to deny it, but he didn't say anything.

"You're through, Rouen," I said. "Eddie didn't kill me. He is under arrest right now and he's got one bullet through his shoulder and one through his hand. From my gun. So here I am, Rouen. You want me dead so bad, I guess you'll have to do your own dirty work."

He quickly brought his hands up from his lap and put them on the desk. He shook his head. "You've forgotten, Mr. March, that I told you I abhor violence in any form."

"Sure you do," I said, "You don't mind it as long as you can order it and then you can look at your beautiful house while it's being done. But you can't stand to face what you do, can you?"

He didn't say anything. He was staring at me, his face working nervously.

"You're all through," I told him again. "I came up to tell you. Your boy West Carroll is under arrest for murder. The rest of your gang will be rounded up. Sure, maybe one or two will escape and maybe you got away with the last batch of heroin, but you're through. Your partners aren't going to like it, Rouen. They hate failure, and I doubt if they will be your partners any longer. You probably won't be arrested yourself, but the whole city of New Orleans and the country are going to know about you. That you were nothing but a dirty drug peddler—that all of this is built on the souls and bodies of your drug addicts. All of the people here who you've thought of as your inferiors are going to look at you after this and spit. ... Do you know what I would do if I were you, Rouen?"

"No," he said. His voice was so low I could hardly hear it.

"I'd put a bullet through my own head," I said. I looked at him again and saw that he had suddenly become an old man, sagging in his chair. I turned and walked out of the room.

Back in the Cadillac, I headed for the airport and stepped on the accelerator. I stopped once to make a phone call, then went on. When I got there, it was still twenty-five minutes before flight time. They hadn't opened the gates yet, but the people were lined up, waiting. I walked along the line until I saw her.

"Hello," I said. I could feel the pain inside of me, but I kept it out of my voice.

She looked startled, but she quickly managed a smile. "Milo," she said. "Something came up suddenly and I had to go to New York. I called your hotel, but they said you were out."

"Sure," I said. "You've got a few minutes. Step out of the line so I can at least say good-bye properly."

She left the line and walked around the railing to me. She was carrying an overnight bag.

"That all the luggage you're taking?" I asked.

"No, my suitcase is checked on the flight," she said. Her eyes were searching my face as though she sensed something different.

"I'll miss you," I said.

"I'll be back soon," she said. "I'll miss you, too."

"Will you?" I asked. "Will you miss me all those long days and nights you're in prison?"

Then fear came alive in her eyes.

"I was slow, wasn't I?" I said. "All the little things I missed. Like on the plane when you only got real friendly after you found out I was coming to work on the case of the two men who had been killed. Like I kept wondering how Eddie Capo knew I was in New Orleans and why, almost as soon as I got here. Like I mention to you that I think the case is tied in with narcotics, and when I go to see Rouen and tell him what I think he's doing, only I left out drugs, he reminded me that I must think he was in that, too. Or like the fact that I mention to you the other night that I expected to get the killer, and within ten minutes after I leave you, Eddie Capo is racing to tell West Carroll that I'm coming after him. Eddie knew what he was talking about when he called me sucker, didn't he?"

"Milo … ," she said, but the rest of the words stuck in her throat.

"Was that all it was?" I asked harshly. "Were all the good times, the closeness when you were in my arms, the way your lips and body clung to mine—was it all just good business?"

"No, Milo," she said. "It was at first, but not later." There were tears in her eyes, but how could I be sure they were real?

"Did you have a lot of laughs with the others?" I asked. "Talking about how poor, dumb March was panting to go to the slaughter? Did Eddie Capo promise to bring you some of my blood as a souvenir when he killed me?"

"No," she cried.

"How does it feel," I asked, "to lie all night in the arms of a man you're going to have killed? Does it make it more exciting? Does it give you an extra thrill?"

She shook her head, her blond hair flying about her head.

While I'd been talking, Lieutenant Stern and one of the Federal men had come up behind her. I looked at them. "Did you get her luggage?" I asked.

"Yes," Stern said. "We phoned and had them hold it."

She stiffened at the sound of his voice, but she didn't turn around.

"I think you'll find the heroin in one of her bags," I said. "Probably the one she's carrying. One of those addresses Perrin went to was a drop for her. Maybe Royal Street. She was the courier to New York. You'll be able to get further identification, if you need it, from Lew Manton. He's the one the New York police have and he's anxious to sing. He was following her the night I met her."

I took a last, long look at her. She was still beautiful.

"Take her away," I said wearily.

The Federal man took her by the arm and they started walking across the terminal with her.

"Lieutenant," I called. Stern looked around. "I'll be going back to New York tomorrow. But let me know and I'll come back when you need my testimony."

He nodded and they went on. I watched until they were out of sight.

I went out to the Cadillac and drove back to the hotel. I went up to my room. From the looks of it, the lab men had already been there. I picked up the phone and put in a long-distance call to Martin Raymond.

"Milo," he said, coming on, "I was wondering when I was going to hear from you."

"Well, you've heard," I said. "The case is all wrapped up. The murder is solved and a drug ring broken up. You have, by hiring me, made a great contribution to law and order."

"Drugs?" he said. "You mean those men were mixed up with a drug ring?"

"Not at all," I said. "They were innocent bystanders. ... Oh, yes, I'm afraid you'll have to pay out the full hundred and fifty thousand dollars. I didn't save you a dime."

"Well," he said weakly, "you can't win them all."

"That's my boy who said that," I said. "What's more, you owe me nine hundred dollars for not saving you a dime. But there's one very good piece of news for you."

"What's that?"

"I think you'll get some of the expense money back. Let me see. I now have plane fare back and perhaps another hundred dollars left. There will still be a doctor's bill to pay and a new shirt to buy, and then I expect to spend some money tonight. But I think I'll have twenty or thirty dollars to give back to you. I'll send my check for it along with the bill. That'll help offset the one hundred and fifty-one thousand, eight hundred dollars it's costing you. Tell the Board of Directors to run that up the flagpole and see who salutes it."

"Milo," he asked anxiously, "are you drunk?"

"No," I said. "But if you call back in an hour, I will be."

I hung up and went downstairs to keep my word.

A MILO MARCH BIBLIOGRAPHY

This bibliography of novels, novelets, and stories is organized chronologically, by the date of initial publication in
hardcover in the United States. All of the novels were also
published in Canada; sixteen were published in the United
Kingdom as well (the exceptions are *Hangman's Harvest, As
Old as Cain, A Man in the Middle, Wild Midnight Falls, Born
to Be Hanged*, and *Death to the Brides*). A complete publishing history for each book appears in the Steeger Books series
on the book's copyright page.

1952

Hangman's Harvest
  New York: Henry Holt Co., February 1952.
  Toronto: Clarke, Irwin & Co., 1952.
  New York: Popular Library #482, 1953, as *Don't Get
    Caught.*
  New York: Paperback Library #16, January 1971. Cover by
    Robert McGinnis.
  Steeger Books, 2020. Milo March Mystery #1.

"The Jelly Roll Heist." *Popular Detective*, September 1952.

"Assignment: Red Berlin." *Bluebook,* December 1952. Illustrated by Bill Fleming. A condensed version of *No Grave for March* (1953).

1953

All the Way Down. New York: Popular Library #530, 1953. Original title: *No Grave for March.*

Don't Get Caught. New York: Popular Library #482, 1953. Original title: *Hangman's Harvest* (1952).

No Grave for March
New York: Henry Holt & Co., January 1953.
Toronto: Clarke, Irwin & Co., 1953.
New York: Popular Library #530, 1953, as *All the Way Down.*
London: Eyre & Spottiswoode, 1954.
London: Corgi Books T160, 1956. Cover by John Richards.
New York: Paperback Library #13 (63-440), October 1970. Cover by Robert McGinnis.
Steeger Books, 2020. Milo March Mystery #2.

"Hair the Color of Blood." *Bluebook,* July 1953. Illustrated by Al Tarter.

"The Hot Ice Blues." *Bluebook,* September 1953. Illustrated by Stan Drake.

"Murder for Madame." *Popular Detective,* Fall 1953.

"The Man Inside." *Bluebook,* December 1953. Illustrated by Al Tarter. A condensation of the 1954 book version.

1954

The Man Inside
  Magazine story: See "The Man Inside" (1953).
  New York: Henry Holt & Co., February 1954. Dust jacket by Ben Feder, Inc.
  Toronto: George J. McLeod, 1954.
  New York: Popular Library #632, 1954, as *Now It's My Turn.* Cover by Ray Johnson.
  London: Eyre & Spottiswoode, 1955.
  New York: Popular Library Giant #G282, 1958. Cover by Ray Johnson.
  Movie: *The Man Inside* (UK, 1958), directed by John Gilling, starring Jack Palance and Anita Ekberg. Screenplay by David Shaw, based on the novel.
  New York: Paperback Library #4 (63-213), January1970. Cover by Robert McGinnis.
  Steeger Books, 2020. Milo March Mystery #3.

Now It's My Turn. New York: Popular Library #632, 1954. Original title: *The Man Inside.*

As Old as Cain
  New York: Henry Holt & Co., October 1954.

Toronto: George J. McLeod, 1954.

New York: Mercury Publications, Bestseller Mystery #B202, 1957, as *Take One for Murder*. Cover design by George Salter.

New York: Paperback Library #17 (63-527), February1971. Cover by Robert McGinnis.

Steeger Books, 2020. Milo March Mystery #4.

1955

The Splintered Man

New York: Rinehart & Co., November 1955.

Toronto: Clarke, Irwin & Co., November 1955.

New York: Mystery Guild, March 1956.

London: T.V. Boardman (American Bloodhound Espionage Mystery #145), 1957. Dust jacket by Denis McLoughlin.

New York: Permabook #M-3080, April 1957. Cover by Robert Schultz.

New York: Paperback Library #7 (63-306), April 1970. Cover by Robert McGinnis.

Steeger Books, 2020. Milo March Mystery #5.

1956

A Lonely Walk

New York: Rinehart & Co., October 1956.

Toronto: Clarke, Irwin & Co., 1956.

London: T.V. Boardman (American Bloodhound Mystery #177), 1957. Dust jacket by Denis McLoughlin.

New York: Ace Double #D-225, 1957. Cover by Rudy Nappi.

Magazine: "The Bodies Beautiful of Rome." *Cavalier,* July 1957. Illustrated by Bob Schulze. A condensed version.

New York: Paperback Library #12 (63-1421), September 1970. Cover by Robert McGinnis.

Steeger Books, 2020. Milo March Mystery #6.

1957

"The Bodies Beautiful of Rome." *Cavalier,* July 1957. Illustrated by Bob Schulze. A condensed version of *A Lonely Walk.*

Take One for Murder. New York: Mercury Publications, Bestseller Mystery #B202, 1957. Original title: *As Old as Cain.*

1958

The Gallows Garden

New York: Rinehart & Co., February 1958.

Toronto: Clarke, Irwin & Co., 1958.

London: T.V. Boardman (American Bloodhound Mystery #225), 1958.

New York: Pocket Books #1240, May 1959, as *The Lady Came to Kill.* Cover by Len Goldberg.

New York: Paperback Library #18 (63-549), March 1971. Cover by Robert McGinnis.

Steeger Books, 2020. Milo March Mystery #7.

A Hearse of Another Color

New York: Holt, Rinehart & Co., August 1958.

Toronto: Clarke, Irwin & Co., July 1958.

London: T.V. Boardman (American Bloodhound Mystery #253), 1959.

New York: Pocket Books #1259, September 1959. Cover by James Meese.

Serialized as "A Hearse of Another Colour" in *Suspense* (UK: Fleetwood Publications), May 1960 and June 1960. Illustrated by W. Langhammer.

London: Corgi Books #972, 1961. Cover by James. E. McConnell.

New York: Paperback Library #15 (63-486), December 1970. Cover by Robert McGinnis.

Steeger Books, 2020. Milo March Mystery #8.

1959

So Dead the Rose

New York: Rinehart & Co., February 1959.

Toronto: Clarke, Irwin & Co., 1959.

London: T.V. Boardman (American Bloodhound Mystery #286), 1960.

New York: Pocket Books #1274, March 1960. Cover by Jerry Allison.

New York: Paperback Library #11 (63-396), August 1970. Cover by Robert McGinnis.

Steeger Books, 2020. Milo March Mystery #9.

The Lady Came to Kill. New York: Pocket Books #1240, May 1959. Cover by Len Goldberg. Original title: *The Gallows Garden.*

1961

"The Red, Red Flowers." *Bluebook,* February 1961.

"The Twisted Trap." *Bluebook,* June 1961. Illustrated by Harvey Kidder.

1962

Jade for a Lady
New York: Holt, Rinehart & Winston, March 1962.
Toronto: Holt, Rinehart & Winston of Canada, 1962.
London: T.V. Boardman (American Bloodhound Mystery #399), 1962.
Roslyn, NY: Walter J. Black, Inc., July 1962. Detective Book Club #243.
New York: Paperback Library #1 (63-204), January 1970. Cover by Robert McGinnis.
Steeger Books, 2020. Milo March Mystery #10.

1963

Softly in the Night
New York: Holt, Rinehart & Winston, February 1963. Dust

jacket by Ben Feder, Inc.

Toronto: Holt, Rinehart & Winston of Canada, 1963.

London: T.V. Boardman (American Bloodhound Mystery #433), 1963. Dust jacket by Denis McLoughlin.

York: Paperback Library #6 (63-288), March 1970. Cover by Robert McGinnis.

Steeger Books, 2020. Milo March Mystery #11.

1964

Uneasy Lies the Dead

New York: Holt, Rinehart & Winston, January1964. Dust jacket by Ben Feder, Inc.

Toronto: Holt, Rinehart & Winston of Canada, 1964.

London: T.V. Boardman (American Bloodhound Mystery #470), 1964.

New York: Paperback Library #8 (63-328), May 1970. Cover by Robert McGinnis.

Steeger Books, 2020. Milo March Mystery #12.

Six Who Ran

New York: Holt, Rinehart & Winston, July 1964.

Toronto: Holt, Rinehart & Winston of Canada, 1964.

London: T.V. Boardman (American Bloodhound Mystery #498), 1965.

Roslyn, NY: Walter J. Black, Inc., December 1964. Detective Book Club #272.

New York: Paperback Library #10 (63-380), July 1970. Cover by Robert McGinnis.

Steeger Books, 2020. Milo March Mystery #13.

1965

Wanted: Dead Men
New York: Holt, Rinehart & Winston, November 1965. Dust
jacket by Ben Feder, Inc.
Toronto: Holt, Rinehart & Winston of Canada, November
1965.
London: T.V. Boardman (American Bloodhound Mystery
#528), 1966.
New York: Paperback Library #14 (63-460), November
1970. Cover by Robert McGinnis.
Steeger Books, 2020. Milo March Mystery #14.

1966

The Day It Rained Diamonds
New York: Holt, Rinehart & Winston, October 1966.
Toronto: Holt, Rinehart & Winston of Canada, 1966.
London: MacDonald (A Boardman Mystery), 1968.
New York: Paperback Library #3 (63-231), January 1970.
Cover by Robert McGinnis.
Steeger Books, 2020. Milo March Mystery #15.

1967

A Man in the Middle
New York: Holt, Rinehart & Winston, August 1967.

Toronto: Holt, Rinehart & Winston of Canada, 1967.

Roslyn, NY: Walter J. Black, Inc., January 1968. Detective Book Club #309.

New York: Paperback Library #2 (63-203), January 1970. Cover by Robert McGinnis.

Steeger Books, 2020. Milo March Mystery #16.

1968

Wild Midnight Falls

New York: Holt, Rinehart & Winston, August 1968. Dust jacket by James McMullen.

Toronto: Holt, Rinehart & Winston of Canada, June 1968.

Roslyn, NY: Walter J. Black, Inc., October 1968. Detective Book Club #318.

New York: Paperback Library #5 (63-265), February1970. Cover by Robert McGinnis.

Steeger Books, 2020. Milo March Mystery #17.

1969

The Flaming Man

New York: Holt, Rinehart & Winston, February 1969. Dust jacket by Pete Plascencia.

Toronto: Holt, Rinehart & Winston of Canada, 1969.

London: Robert Hale, 1970.

New York: Paperback Library #9 (63-353), June 1970. Cover by Robert McGinnis.

Steeger Books, 2020. Milo March Mystery #18.

1970

Green Grow the Graves

New York: Holt, Rinehart & Winston, February 1970. Dust jacket by Stan Zagorski.

Toronto: Holt, Rinehart & Winston of Canada, February 1970.

London: Robert Hale, April 1971.

New York: Paperback Library #19 (63-568), April 1971. Cover by Robert McGinnis.

Steeger Books, 2020. Milo March Mystery #19.

1971

The Bonded Dead

New York: Holt, Rinehart & Winston, April 1971.

Toronto: Holt, Rinehart & Winston of Canada, 1971.

Roslyn, NY: Walter J. Black, Inc., July 1971. Detective Book Club #351.

New York: Paperback Library #24 (64-684), September 1971. Cover by Robert McGinnis.

London: Robert Hale, 1973.

Steeger Books, 2020. Milo March Mystery #20.

1973

Born to Be Hanged

New York: Holt, Rinehart & Winston, August 1973. Dust jacket by Jay Smith.

Toronto: Holt, Rinehart & Winston of Canada, 1973.

Roslyn, NY: Walter J. Black, Inc., November 1973. Detective Book Club #379.

Steeger Books, 2020. Milo March Mystery #21.

2020

Death to the Brides

First edition: Steeger Books, 2020. Milo March Mystery #22.

Unpublished manuscript, 1975, in the Howard Gotlieb Archival Research Center, Boston University.

The Twisted Trap: Six Milo March Stories

First edition: Steeger Books, 2020. Milo March Mystery #23. Contents:

"The Jelly Roll Heist." *Popular Detective*, September 1952.

"Assignment: Red Berlin." *Bluebook*, December 1952.

"Hair the Color of Blood." *Bluebook*, July 1953.

"The Hot Ice Blues." *Bluebook*, September 1953.

"Murder for Madame." *Popular Detective*, Fall 1953.

"The Man Inside." *Bluebook*, December 1953.

"The Bodies Beautiful of Rome." *Cavalier*, July 1957.

"The Red, Red Flowers." *Bluebook*, February 1961.

"The Twisted Trap." *Bluebook*, June 1961.

ABOUT THE AUTHOR

Kendell Foster Crossen (1910–1981), the only child of Samuel Richard Crossen and Clo Foster Crossen, was born on a farm outside Albany in Athens County, Ohio—a village of some 550 souls in the year of this birth. His ancestors on his mother's side include the 19th-century songwriter Stephen Collins Foster ("Oh! Susanna"); William  Allen, founder of Allentown, Pennsylvania; and Ebenezer Foster, one of the Minute Men who sprang to arms at the Lexington alarm in April 1775.

Ken went to Rio Grande College on a football scholarship but stayed only one year. "When I was fairly young, I developed the disgusting habit of reading," says Milo March, and it seems Ken Crossen, too, preferred self-education. He loved literature and poetry; favorite authors included Christopher Marlowe and Robert Service. He also enjoyed participant sports and was a semi-pro fighter in the heavyweight class. He became a practicing magician and had a passion for chess.

After college Ken wrote several one-act plays that were produced in a small Cleveland theater. He worked in steel mills and Fisher Body plants. Then he was employed as an insurance investigator, or "claims adjuster," in Cleveland. But he left the job and returned to the theater, now as a performer: a tumbling clown in the Tom Mix Circus; a comic and carnival barker for a tent show, and an actor in a medicine show.

In 1935, Ken hitchhiked to New York City with a typewriter under his arm, and found work with the WPA Writers' Project, covering cricket for the *New York City Guidebook.* In 1936, he was hired by the Munsey Publishing Company as associate editor of the popular *Detective Fiction Weekly.* The company asked him to come up with a character to compete with The Shadow, and thus was born a unique superhero of pulps, comic books, and radio—The Green Lama, an American mystic trained in Tibetan Buddhism.

Crossen sold his first story, "The Aaron Burr Murder Case," to *Detective Fiction Weekly* in September 1939, but says he didn't begin to make a living from writing till 1941. He tried his hand at publishing true crime magazines, comics, and a picture magazine, without great success, so he set out for Hollywood. From his typewriter flowed hundreds of stories, short novels for magazines, scripts radio, television, and film, nonfiction articles. He delved into science fiction in the 1950s, starting with "Restricted Clientele" (February 1951). His dystopian novels *Year of Consent* and *The Rest Must Die* also appeared in this decade.

In the course of his career Ken Crossen acquired six pseudonyms: Richard Foster, Bennett Barlay, Kent Richards, Clay Richards, Christopher Monig, and M.E. Chaber. The variety was necessary because different publishers wanted to reserve specific bylines for their own publications. Ken based "M.E. Chaber" on the Hebrew word for "author," *mechaber.*

In the early '50s, as M.E. Chaber, Crossen began to write a series of full-length mystery/espionage novels featuring Milo March, an insurance investigator. The first, *Hangman's Harvest,* was published in 1952. In all, there are twenty-two Milo March novels. One, *The Man Inside,* was made into a British film starring Jack Palance.

Most of Ken's characters were private detectives, and Milo was the most popular. Paperback Library reissued twenty-five Crossen titles in 1970–1971, with covers by Robert McGinnis. Twenty were Milo March novels, four featured an insurance investigator named Brian Brett, and one was about CIA agent Kim Locke.

Crossen excelled at producing well-plotted entertainment with fast-moving action. His research skills were a strong asset, back when research meant long hours searching library microfilms and poring over street maps and hotel floorplans. His imagination took him to many international hot spots, although he himself never traveled abroad. Like Milo March, he hated flying ("When you've seen one cloud, you've seen them all").

Ken Crossen was married four times. With his first wife he had three children (Stephen, Karen, Kendra) and with his second a son (David). He lived in New York, Florida, Southern California, Nevada, and other parts of the country. Milo March moves from Denver to New York City after five books of the series, with an apartment on Perry Street in Greenwich Village; that's where Ken lived, too. His and Milo's favorite watering hole was the Blue Mill Tavern, a short walk from the apartment.

Ken Crossen was a combination of many of the traits of his different male characters: tough, adventuresome, with a taste for gin and shapely women. But perhaps the best observation was made in an obituary written by sci-fi writer Avram Davidson, who described Ken as a fundamentally gentle person who had been buffeted by many winds.

www.ingramcontent.com/pod-product-compliance
Lightning Source LLC
Chambersburg PA
CBHW032042240626
47154CB00003B/1029